'*Sword of Light* ... myth and imagination into a ... mping tale. Rhianna has you on her side long before she rides into battle brandishing Excalibur.' *The Times*

'There is magic at work here as strong as Merlin's.' Mary Hoffman, author of *David*

'This is a book packed with excitement as the evil shadrake would not look out of place in *Lord of the Rings*, and with the promise of three more volumes in the Pendragon Legacy, a treat for all lovers of adventure and fantasy.' *Carousel*

'It's fantastic, so accessible… I loved it!' *The Bookette*

'A cracking page-turning adventure… Utterly gripping.' *lovereading4kids.co.uk*

'This is a wonderful, magical, mythical, historical adventure. I loved Rhianna as a feisty tomboyish heroine (think Katniss on a magic horse).' *Books, ... gging*

SWORD OF LIGHT

PENDRAGON LEGACY
BOOK 1

SWORD
OF
LIGHT

KATHERINE ROBERTS

templar

A TEMPLAR BOOK

First published in the UK in 2012 by Templar Publishing,
This paperback edition published in 2012 by Templar
Publishing, an imprint of The Templar Company Limited,
Deepdene Lodge, Deepdene Avenue, Dorking,
Surrey, RH5 4AT, UK
www.templarco.co.uk

First paperback edition
1 3 5 7 9 10 8 6 4 2

ISBN 978-1-84877-393-6

Printed and bound by CPI Group (UK) Ltd, Croydon, CR0 4YY

For Mary

Contents

Characters

ALBA – Rhianna's mist horse, a white mare
from Avalon.

ARIANRHOD – Rhianna's maid, ex-maid of
Morgan Le Fay. Her cheek bears a scar
in the shape of a pentacle.

CAI – young squire at Camelot who becomes
Rhianna's champion.

CHIEF CYNRIC – leader of the Saxons.

ELPHIN – Prince of Avalon and only son of
Lord Avallach.

EVENSTAR – Elphin's mist horse, a white
stallion from Avalon.

GARETH – older squire, Cai's rival.

KING ARTHUR – king of Britain. His ghost
   appears to Rhianna while his body
   sleeps in Avalon awaiting rebirth.

LADY ISABEL – lady in charge of the damsels
   at Camelot.

LORD AVALLACH – Lord of Avalon and
   Elphin's father. Leader of the Wild Hunt.

MERLIN – King Arthur's druid. Since he is
   half Avalonian, he can work magic in
   the world of men.

MORDRED – Rhianna's cousin and rival for
   the throne; the son of Morgan Le Fay.

MORGAN LE FAY – King Arthur's sister and
   Mordred's mother, a witch. Now dead,
   her spirit advises Mordred from Annwn.

NIMUE – the Lady of the Lake, who takes
   Excalibur after Arthur's death.

Characters

QUEEN GUINEVERE – Rhianna's mother,
   whereabouts unknown.
RHIANNA PENDRAGON – daughter of King
   Arthur, raised in Avalon.
SANDY – Cai's pony, rescued from the Saxons.
SIR AGRAVAINE – grumpy older knight.
SIR BEDIVERE – a younger knight, also known as
   'Soft Hands' because of his gentle nature.
SIR BORS – leader of King Arthur's knights.
SIR LANCELOT – Arthur's champion knight.
THE SHADRAKE – a dragon from Annwn,
   breathes ice instead of fire and hunts
   between worlds.

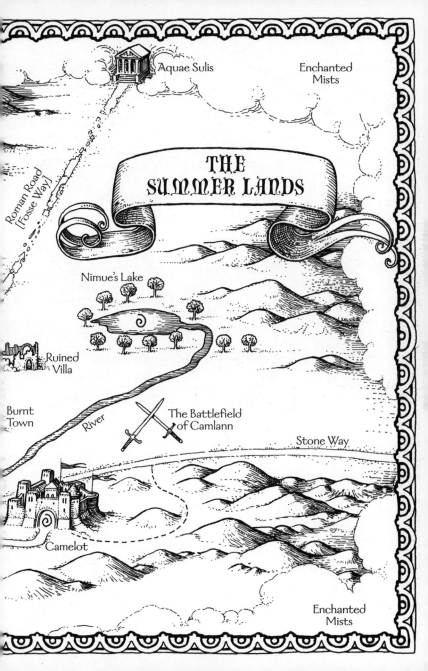

Four Lights stand against the dark:
The Sword Excalibur that was
forged in Avalon,
The Lance of Truth made by the
hands of men,
The Crown of Dreams, which hides
the jewel of Annwn,
And the Grail said to hold all the
stars in heaven.

THE DARK
KNIGHT WAKES

The day after he had killed King Arthur,
Mordred opened his eyes to flickering
candlelight and damp rock. There had been
nightmares, screaming and much pain.
Terrible pain such as his pampered body had
never felt before. But the worst had passed.
His crippled form stirred in the shadows and
his remaining hand closed about cold metal.
Not his axe – he'd lost that on the battlefield,
along with his right hand – but a magic
mirror his mother had given him before she
left the world of men.

He breathed on the black glass, and her image swirled to life. Raven haired and beautiful, she looked at least twenty years younger than when she had died.

"Who commands the Grail?" he demanded.

His mother's face flickered. "The one called Pendragon."

"So it serves *me* now?" Mordred said, impatient. Even dead, his mother could be annoyingly vague.

"I'm not sure. It's unclear… I see a girl, a daughter…"

Mordred flung the mirror across the cave. "No!" he roared. "Arthur had no daughter! We would have known."

He'd won the battle. He'd killed Arthur Pendragon, high king of men and guardian of the Round Table. Even now, his spies were

looking for the Sword and the Lance.
The Crown, snatched by a dragon from his
uncle's corpse on the battlefield, was rightfully
his. As soon as he got his hands – *hand*,
curse it – on the Grail, he would be strong
and handsome again, and the world would
worship at his feet. But now this! Another
with a claim to the throne.

Clenching his teeth against the pain,
he rolled off the rocky shelf that served as
his bed. He could not walk because his stupid
horse had fallen on him and crushed one of
his legs. He crawled across the floor, the
bandaged stump of his arm leaving a trail
of blood. The mirror had cracked, making
a jagged line across his mother's face to
match the scar Arthur's sword had left
across his own.

"Where?" he hissed. "Where is she? She must die!"

The witch's face blurred, becoming old and then young again.

"Beyond our reach in Avalon. But not for much longer, I think."

"What do you mean? Speak plainly, woman!"

His mother smiled. "I mean, Mordred my beautiful son, that you need to be patient for once. Heal. Grow strong again. Be crafty like the dragon that waits in its lair. Let the girl come to you. They took the king's body through the enchanted mists. If she has a drop of Arthur's blood in her body, she will come. And then you can kill her – or enslave her, as you wish. She's only a damsel, after all. She's grown up in a crystal palace where there

is no disease or death, protected by magic.
The world of men will be a shock to her.
She's hardly going to lead the knights in
battle, is she? How much of a threat can
she be?"

◄◙ 1 ◙►

Pendragon

A maiden lives in Avalon's hall
Her spirit the purest of them all.
Brave of heart and hair aflame,
Mortal damsel with secret name.

Rhianna crouched over her horse's neck to duck another low branch. Twigs snatched at her braid, pulling out a few copper strands and making her eyes water. All around her in the golden wood she could see pale blurs as her rivals misted to avoid the trees. Being one of the Avalonian herd, whose coats shone like the moon, Alba could do that too, of course. But if Rhianna let the mare mist like the other horses, she would fall off and everyone would laugh at her.

She urged Alba alongside Prince Elphin's little Evenstar. "What's the matter?" she called as they galloped side by side. "Afraid you'll hit a tree?"

Her friend shouted something back that she didn't catch. She saw the air sparkle as he flicked a branch out of the way, and grinned as he dropped behind.

I can go faster, Alba said, excited by galloping with the herd.

"Go on, then!" Rhianna told the mare.

She overtook two of the Avalonian girls, scared herself by slipping sideways as Alba swerved around another tree, and grabbed the mane to pull herself back on board. Her blood pounded with excitement as she saw the glint of water through the leaves. She'd win today, if she kept her nerve. The mist magic took time to work, and the others would not dare gallop so fast through the wood without it. The worst she'd have to worry about would be a few apples thrown at her as she passed the leaders.

She risked raising her head. The beach led to an ancient jetty that disappeared into the mist, where they'd agreed to finish the race. That was the furthest they could go without crossing the enchanted sea that kept the Isle of Avalon hidden from the world of men.

The thrill of their wild gallop faded slightly. More than anything else, Rhianna wanted to visit the world of men and look for her real parents. But nobody would tell her who they were, or even if they were still alive, and her pleas for someone to take her through the mists fell on deaf ears. One day she might swim across the water on her own. That would show everyone—

Path blocked! Alba whinnied as a sharp twig poked her in the chest.

Rhianna hauled desperately on the reins as she saw the fallen tree, too high to jump. She flattened herself alongside Alba's neck and felt the little horse begin to mist under her. Then a branch smacked her between the eyes, and the world went dark.

❧❧

A shadow stirred in the darkness. Someone was whispering. It sounded like a question:

"Who commands the Grail?" She had a terrifying glimpse of bloodstained rock.

Then she heard singing, and the light returned.

"Rhia? Rhianna?" Elphin sounded scared. "Wake up now, please!"

She opened her eyes and blinked up at the violet sky through a curtain of falling leaves. Bright autumn sunlight dappled her legs. Apples lay all around. Alba's soft muzzle nibbled her ear. *Sorry*, breathed the mare. A sweet scent surrounded her – the smell of magic. It must have been Elphin she'd heard singing in her dream.

She sat up with a groan and touched her forehead. Her fingers came away sticky with blood, and her head throbbed. She managed a grin for her friend. As the only human of her age in Avalon, Rhianna had put up with a lot of teasing over the years. The other children made fun of her hands, with only four fingers and a thumb on each, of her red hair, of the freckles on her nose, of her loud voice that murdered the ancient songs, and – most of all – of her failure to master even a glimmer of magic despite being surrounded by it every day of her life. But Elphin never teased her like the others did. Maybe because he didn't have any brothers or sisters of his own, Lord Avallach's son had always looked after her as if she were his real sister.

"Suppose I didn't win today, then?" Her voice came out croaky.

Relief flashed in her friend's eyes, which had turned purple with concern. He ran a hand through his dark curls, and his extra fingers twitched as if they longed for his harp. "I think the mists opened," he said. "There was a strange shadow. Then you fell off."

Rhianna shook her head – a mistake. Leaves and sky spun around her, making her feel a bit sick.

"I was knocked off," she insisted. "That's different. I haven't fallen off for ages, not since I learned how to talk to Alba." She looked at the beach, where the other mist horses were pawing at the sand while their riders crowded around the jetty, pointing at something out on the water. "Why didn't you carry on? You might have beaten me, for once."

"And leave you lying here? Don't be silly. The race isn't that important."

She grinned again. "That's why you never win."

Elphin sighed. "You're crazy, Rhia. Galloping

so fast through the woods without even any magic to clear the branches out of your way! Why do you do it? What if Alba had misted around a tree, and you'd broken your neck?"

"Then your people would just sing it better again, wouldn't they?" Rhianna said.

But she felt bad when she looked at her mare. Alba's beautiful silver head hung low. Her flanks heaved, dark with sweat. Elphin was right. She must try to think a bit more of others. What if he had been the one to get knocked off his horse while looking out for her? There would be no chance of his father letting her visit the world of men then.

"A broken neck needs more than a simple healing song," Elphin said, serious. "You'd have to sleep for many years in the crystal caverns until we got your soul back into your body, and when you woke up I'd be an old man."

Rhianna pulled a face. "It might be worth it! At least I'd get to see your mysterious caverns, then." Despite many attempts, she'd never managed to get past the magic that protected the deeper levels of Lord Avallach's palace.

Elphin frowned. "That's not funny. Anyway, there's a boat at the jetty. It's just as well you fell off, or you and Alba would probably have galloped straight off the end and sunk it. We'd best go back to the palace and tell Father we've got visitors. Then I can get my harp and play away your headache. Can you ride, do you think?"

"Of course I can ride. Takes more than a little tap like that to bother me. And I haven't got a headache." The last part was a lie, though, because she did have. A horrid, pounding, human one. She leaned against Alba's neck, stroking the pale mane, still a bit dizzy. There had been something about a grail, whatever that was...

Maybe you had better lead me? said the mare.

"Don't be silly. Humans are tougher than you think."

She ignored Elphin's offered hand and looked around for a log to stand on. As she climbed on it, she saw what the others on the beach were all looking at. A small boat had come out of the mist. When it reached the shallows, a man in a hooded grey robe jumped into the water. Her skin prickled. Not an Avalonian – Elphin's people hated getting their feet wet. The man was tall, even for a human, and looked familiar.

"It's Merlin!" Grinning, she jumped off the

log and led Alba towards the beach. "You go back for your harp, if you want," she called. "Something important must have happened in the world of men."

Elphin made a face. But he pulled his reins over his horse's ears and followed.

The Avalonians crowded curiously around the boat, while the old druid stowed his oars and rubbed his back. Rhianna braced herself for the others' taunts. But when she led Alba out of the trees, everyone fell silent and stepped back to let her and Elphin pass.

Merlin lowered his hood to reveal a straggly white beard braided with falcon feathers. He turned a pale blue gaze on them. "Might have known it wouldn't take you two very long to show up," he muttered.

"*Faha'ruh*, Merlin." Elphin said, raising

his hand to his forehead in the formal Avalonian greeting.

Merlin frowned. "Growing up as well, I see. Let's save the ceremonial stuff for later, shall we? There's no time to waste if my journey's not going to be in vain."

Rhianna watched the old druid warily. He often visited to check up on her, appearing unannounced out of the mists and then disappearing again just as suddenly with no explanation. Usually, he looked at her as if she were an annoying bit of dirt he'd picked up on his sandal. Today his pale eyes had pity in them. A bit embarrassed, she touched the bump on her forehead. Was it still bleeding? But Merlin was not looking at her head. He was looking into the boat, like everyone else.

Elphin let out a little hum of sadness.

Rhianna looked into the boat, too, and saw a man lying in the bottom. He had been partly covered by a battered shield with a red dragon painted on it, but she could see terrible wounds beneath. His head rested on a folded cloak, stiff with dried blood. His hair fanned out, faded chestnut streaked with grey. His hands were folded on his breast above the shield, and his boots still had mud on them. Yellow mud, a different colour from Avalon's rich dark earth.

All this she saw, before Merlin dug his gnarled fingers into her shoulder and said, "Young Mordred finally killed him! So now you're our only hope. A slip of a girl. God help us all!"

The others looked sideways at her. A few of the Avalonian girls giggled nervously. Whatever else Rhianna might be, she was no 'slip'.

Rhianna had been feeling a bit envious of the dead man in the boat, and wondered who he might be. A hero of some sort, obviously. Only great heroes were allowed through the enchanted mists to Avalon when they died. One day, when he was ready to be reborn, he would join the Wild Hunt that rode into the world of men to collect stray souls – while she would still be stuck here.

Suddenly, she was fed up with everyone laughing at her. Fed up with all of them thinking she would never be any good because she was a human with a terrible voice, the wrong number of fingers and no magic.

"I'm not a slip!" she said, drawing herself up to her full height and shrugging off the druid's hand. "I'm taller than everyone else on this beach – except you and whoever that is lying in your boat. "I'm strong enough to swim all the way round the island, fit enough to dance all night, and I can ride faster than anybody in Avalon. Ask Elphin! I usually win our races."

I am very fast, Alba added.

Merlin glanced at her friend, who flushed and mumbled something about her not winning today. The druid looked closely at Rhianna, noticing the blood on her forehead for the first time. He frowned and spread a hand in front of her eyes. "How many fingers?"

She wasn't going to fall for that trick. "Four!" she said. Merlin might work magic like an Avalonian, but he had human hands. Inherited them from his human mother, apparently... a girl like her, but now long dead, who had grown up in Avalon never knowing her real family. She wouldn't let that happen to her.

Merlin grunted. "So we know you can ride faster than anybody else into trees. But can you fight like King Arthur here fought, brave and true to the last, even after his best friend and his own family betrayed him? Can you lead an army of knights against Prince Mordred and his barbarian allies, and hold Camelot against the dark forces of Annwn? Because unless you can do all that, Rhianna Pendragon, the world of men is doomed and the isle of Avalon will soon be lost in the mists for ever."

For the second time that day, Rhianna felt as though she had been knocked flat by a branch. She stared at the dead man in the boat. *Arthur, the greatest king men had ever known.* The Avalonians sang about him all the time. Elphin gave her a concerned look. "Oh Rhia, I'm sorry…"

She felt dizzy again and clutched Alba's mane. "What did you just call me?" she whispered.

"Pendragon! I hope you've not grown deaf as well as foolhardy in my absence." Merlin sighed and lifted the shield out of the boat. He rubbed off a smear of blood, dropped stiffly to one knee and offered the shield to Rhianna. "You, my girl, are the only surviving child of Queen Guinevere and Arthur Pendragon, which makes you heir to the throne of men and guardian of the Round Table. Go on, take the shield. It's yours now, for better or for worse."

While the others gaped at her in astonishment, the druid's lip twitched. "I'm sure there's something you can think of to do with it. Maybe you can use it to stop the tree hitting you next time?"

◁◉ 2 ◉▷

Merlin Sings

The trees wept gold when Merlin brought
   A dying king to the fairy court
   To sing of battles grave and fey
In the world of men where hope once lay.

Rhianna took the shield from the druid and held it awkwardly. It was round, with leather straps at the back for fixing it on to her arm. This battered shield with its red dragon had belonged to her father. It had stopped blows from his enemy's sword – though not all of them, obviously. Some old splinters were stuck in the dragon design. She tried to pull one out, but it wouldn't budge.

Everyone was looking at her as if they expected her to cry. But she hardly ever cried, and she had difficulty thinking of the dead man in the boat as her father. She had no memories of either of her parents. Lord Avallach had been more of a father to her than this dead king… *Arthur Pendragon*! Her head spun. No wonder they hadn't told her the truth. She felt a bit angry they'd waited until he was dead before letting her see him, but she still couldn't find any tears.

Merlin had not moved. The Avalonians were still watching her, whispering uneasily. She didn't know what to do next. Then she realised this could be her chance to see the world of men and find her mother. Queen Guinevere. That made her a princess and Elphin's equal. Nobody could keep her here against her will now. Excitement shivered through her.

"Oh please get up," she said to Merlin, embarrassed. "My father's body can't stay there in your boat like a sack of apples! Elphin, your father should know about this… Does Lord Avallach know who I am?" she asked the druid. She looked forward to seeing the Avalonian lord's face when he found out.

Merlin got up stiffly, wincing as his knees cracked. He gave her an impatient look. "Of course he does! Why do you think old Avallach's looked after you so carefully all these years?"

"I thought it was because I was human and didn't have any magic to stop myself getting hurt," Rhianna said.

To her annoyance, Merlin laughed. "The lord of Avalon has more things to worry about than humans getting hurt," he said. "He merely agreed to hide you. If you'd been a boy, things might have been different. But it's my fault. I should have told you the truth long ago. I've been distracted by Mordred's plots, and time passes so quickly when you get to be as old as I am. I'd still hoped for a son of Arthur's… but it wasn't to be. Ah well, I suppose we'll just have to work with what we've got. The shield's all I have to give you at the moment, I'm afraid. His idiot knights threw Arthur's sword into the lake to stop Mordred's men getting their hands on it, and a dragon stole away his crown." He sighed. "Not that a sword would do you much good, anyway. In your father's world, girls don't fight."

Rhianna's jaw clenched. She was trying to think of a suitable reply, when Elphin cleared his throat and said, "Actually, I think they do. There's a song we sing about women warriors who came to the aid of a great city long ago in the world of men."

Rhianna gave him a grateful look. She didn't remember that one. They couldn't sing it very often. Or maybe Lord Avallach just didn't let them sing it in her presence in case she got dangerous ideas from it? She could believe that. If they had their way, Elphin's parents would wrap her up in enchanted spider webs and never let her out of the palace. "There!" she said. "So I can easily learn to fight, once I've got my father's sword back. Where is this lake? We'd best get going before this Mordred person finds it."

For a heartbeat, Merlin's ice-blue eyes bored into hers. She felt a strange burning inside her head.

Then he laughed again and pointed out into the mists. "The lake that swallowed your father's sword is currently in the middle of a Saxon war camp, out there in the dangerous world of men, far from these calm shores of Avalon. It's no place for a girl, particularly a child of the Pendragon blood. Arthur's body must be taken to the crystal caverns as soon as possible so the process of rebirth can begin. Then maybe we can think what to do about Mordred. The sword will have to be found too, of course, if we're to deal with the dark knight... But we'll discuss this later, when I've had a wash and something to eat. Some of your healing songs wouldn't go amiss, either, Elphin my lad.

The enchantments were difficult this time." He rolled his shoulders and pulled a face at the boat. "Reduced to rowing! I, who once parted the Summer Sea for Arthur and his knights to gallop across and rescue his queen from the Lonely Tor! I'm getting too old for all this gallivanting around between worlds."

Still grumbling, he ordered the Avalonians to make themselves useful and carry Arthur's body to the palace. Then he pulled his staff out of the boat and marched up the beach, the silver spiral at its top glinting as he stabbed it into the sand.

Rhianna and Elphin exchanged a glance. Despite the dead king in the boat and the shock of what Merlin had just told them, they both giggled.

❦

Because of all the songs in the air, news travelled

fast in Avalon. By the time the mist horses reached the palace with their burden, everyone knew of Arthur Pendragon's death and how his own nephew, the dark knight Mordred, had killed him. People lined the path and bowed their heads in silence as the king's body was carried past. Inside the crystal gates, little groups whispered together in the courtyards and gardens. Their songs of sadness made Rhianna's skin prickle. She still couldn't quite believe she was a princess and the daughter of Arthur Pendragon. She kept expecting someone to tell her it was all a big joke.

Merlin and the Avalonians took Arthur's body deep into the underground caverns thick with magic, where no living human foot had ever trod. Elphin hurried after them. Rhianna tried to follow, but as usual found her way blocked by a shimmering rainbow wall that made her feel sleepy just to look at it. She set her jaw and forced herself to step into the shifting colours, determined to see where her father's body was being taken… only to find herself standing in another crystal corridor at the far side of the palace, staring out at an orchard, while some of the boys who had taken part in the race grinned at her. "What's the matter, freckle-face?" they teased. "Lost your way again? You'd think a princess would know her way around a royal palace!" They playfully tugged her braid and ran off.

Cheeks flaming, Rhianna escaped to the stables to groom Alba. The tree she'd galloped into had left a small cut on the mist horse's chest – she'd have to remember to ask Elphin to sing it better later.

"Poor little mare," she whispered, as she energetically brushed the silver coat. "I didn't look where I was going, did I? I promise I'll be more careful when we go to find my father's sword."

Alba nibbled the end of her braid. *I should not have misted. I forgot you are only human.*

Rhianna felt a surge of love for the mare. She put her arms around the silver neck and buried her face into the sweetly scented mane. All at once, everything Merlin had said on the beach caught up with her in a rush. Her father was dead. Murdered by the evil Prince Mordred. She hadn't even known who he was, until too late… Why hadn't they *told* her? Now she would have to wait until his soul was ready to be reborn, and he probably wouldn't recognise her when he woke up. The tears that had not come earlier wet Alba's coat.

"Don't make promises you can't keep, Rhianna Pendragon," said a bell-like voice behind her. "*Careful* won't get you very far in the world of men."

She wiped her eyes before she turned. Elphin's father, Lord Avallach, stood outside the stall, his black hair shadowing his face. She had the feeling he had been there for some time, watching her.

"Hay seed in my eye," she explained quickly. She knew he didn't believe her, though. Not much got past Lord Avallach in his own palace. She wiped her nose on her sleeve and gave him her brightest smile. "Please tell Merlin to let me help him look for my father's sword. I'm not afraid."

Elphin's father came into the stall and picked a twig out of her hair. "I know you're not afraid, my child," he said. "That's what worries me."

She blinked at him in surprise.

"It's true Arthur's sword must be returned to Avalon as soon as possible so we can keep our shores safe from the dark, and only a mortal of the Pendragon bloodline can handle it safely. As far as we know, with Arthur's soul gone from his body, that leaves just two of you – you and Prince Mordred – and for obvious reasons we'd prefer it to be you. Merlin has told me Mordred's gone to ground to lick his wounds, so that gives us some breathing space. But as soon as you leave Avalon, he'll be after you as furiously as my own Wild Hunt goes after the souls of men. You're human. You have no magic, and you've had no training in the arts of war. We've done our best to teach you our ways, but only men can teach you how to fight."

The purple flash in his eyes said the Avalonian lord did not approve of fighting of any sort.

"All the more reason to let me go," Rhianna said, though his words made her stomach flutter. "You can't keep me here, not any more. I'm heir to the throne of men." It still sounded strange, like being in a song.

Lord Avallach sighed. "I know. Which is why I told Merlin he can take you with him when he returns to Camelot. I can't do much to help you once you leave these shores, but I can at least give you a little of our magic to take with you." He snapped his fingers. "Elphin! Bring it in here now."

Rhianna's eyes widened as her friend slipped into the stall, his arms full of silvery material that looked like thousands of tiny moons all folded up together.

He smiled at her as he held it out. "Avalonian armour," he said proudly. "Father's smith made it when he forged Excalibur."

Rhianna frowned, distracted by the glittering tunic. "Forged what?"

"Your father's sword, silly," Elphin said. "Excalibur is its name. All magic swords have names. It was forged here in Avalon to give the Pendragon power over men. That must be why your evil Prince Mordred wants it so badly."

She gave him an irritated look. He seemed to have learned a lot more than she had since they'd returned from the beach. But what did she expect? He was a prince of Avalon and had helped take her father's body to the crystal caverns, whereas she'd only got her hair pulled by stupid boys who did not understand what it felt like to be human.

"Try the armour, child," said Lord Avallach. "I think you'll like it."

Alba sniffed the silvery moons and curled her lip. *It smells funny.*

Rhianna smiled in spite of herself. She raised her arms and crouched so Elphin could slip the armour over her head. It fell in a silvery shower to just above her knees, making a shimmering skirt over her riding leggings. It weighed no more than one of her Avalonian dresses and made no sound when she moved.

"You could dance in that," Lord Avallach said, giving her an approving look. He picked another twig out of her hair and coiled her braid on top of her head. "Mmm, we might make a princess of you yet."

Rhianna flushed. "Thank you," she mumbled, fingering the silver material. "It's perfect."

She picked up the shield, which she'd leaned against Alba's stall, and looped it over her right arm. Twirling on one foot, she clenched her left fist and bared her teeth at Elphin. "But do I look like a *warrior*?"

She laughed as Elphin ducked.

Lord Avallach laughed, too. "Very fierce! But the armour isn't the only magic I'm sending with you. My other gift is standing in front of you."

Rhianna gave Alba a confused look. She'd assumed she would ride her mist mare when they went to look for her father's sword – was that what he meant?

"Me, you idiot," Elphin said, flashing her a bright smile. "Didn't think I'd let you have an exciting adventure in the world of men on your own, did you?"

✣

Rhianna had never seen so many people in Lord Avallach's banqueting hall. Merlin had promised to sing them the tale of King Arthur and Prince Mordred, and all Avalon had come to hear how he thought they might defeat the dark knight. Yet the hall wasn't crowded. The magic of this place meant there was always room for everyone.

Stars glittered through the crystal dome high above their heads, and torches sent rainbows flickering across the floor, so that people danced in a blur of rippling colour. Trees brushed the transparent walls with their leaves so it seemed they were in a woodland glade. Sometimes curious deer and unicorns trotted up to the walls to watch the dancers. Not tonight, though. The wild creatures of Avalon grew nervous when men came through the mists.

Rhianna fidgeted impatiently as the harpists played. Merlin reclined on a couch next to Lord Avallach. The old druid's eyes were closed, and a look of bliss eased the lines on his face. He'd bathed and eaten and rested, so why didn't he just get on with it? While they danced here in Avalon, Mordred might be murdering the rest of her family!

She became aware of people looking sideways at her and raised her chin to stare back at them. She'd made a special effort tonight to honour her dead father. She'd even let the Avalonian girls plait moonflowers into her hair, which made her sneeze, but she left them alone. If she pulled them out, the whole delicate style would only turn into its usual wild mess. She would play the princess on her last night in Avalon. Her last night… The thought made her shiver. But she would be back soon enough with her father's sword, wouldn't she? Then surely they would let her into the crystal caverns to see him.

"I nearly didn't recognise you!" Elphin said, breaking into her thoughts. He crossed his legs and settled his harp in his lap. "Have you still got a headache? I'll play it away now, if you like."

"I'm fine. Stop making such a fuss," Rhianna said. But in truth the girls fiddling with her hair earlier had brought her headache back.

"I'll play anyway, shall I?" Elphin said, and began to strum gently. He flashed her a quick look from under his dark curls. "You don't mind me coming with you, do you?"

"No, of course not."

She'd felt quite relieved when she realised

Lord Avallach meant to send Elphin with her. The idea of being in a strange world with only the grumpy old druid for company had worried her even more than the danger of meeting her cousin Mordred, though she couldn't exactly imagine either Merlin or Elphin fighting at her side if it came to a battle.

"Will your magic work in the world of men?" she asked, suddenly wondering.

Elphin's fingers paused. "I think so. Some of it should, anyway. I'll bring my harp."

Great, Rhianna thought. *That'll be* really *useful in a fight*. But she smiled at him. Her headache had gone. She forgave him for leaving her alone earlier. "Aren't you scared?"

"Are you?"

"Not really."

"Then I'm not, either." Elphin smiled back

at her. "Father wouldn't send me if he thought it was dangerous, would he?"

"I suppose not," Rhianna said. But she eyed Lord Avallach uncertainly, remembering what he'd said about Mordred coming after her like the Wild Hunt.

Elphin gave her a sympathetic look. "Don't worry," he said, mistaking her concern. "Merlin will look after us, won't he? Shh. I think he's going to sing at last."

Rhianna sat up straighter as the druid collected a harp from one of the Avalonians and eased himself down on a stool. He placed his staff carefully between his feet. Flames danced in his pale eyes as he looked her way. He'd changed out of his dirty robe, but his clothes had obviously been borrowed. The leggings were too short, and the tunic sleeves ended just below his elbows. Rhianna frowned. Couldn't her father's druid even bring proper court dress with him to Avalon? Then she remembered he had brought the king's body straight from a battle and felt uneasy again.

Everyone went quiet as Merlin plucked the first note. His voice sounded rough after the sweet Avalonian voices and it wavered with age. But his song had the required magic. It made pictures in the enchanted walls of Avallach's palace so they could all see what he had seen in the world of men.

He sang of a great battle between light and dark. Of King Arthur wielding Excalibur against the gathering storm. Of his knights fighting bravely on their big, strong horses, outnumbered ten to one. Of Mordred's death blow that split the king's helmet from his head.

Of Arthur's final strike that severed Mordred's hand from his arm. Of the dragon that blotted out the sun as it swooped down to steal Arthur's crown from the mud where it had fallen off his broken helmet. Of the rain that came in dark sheets to cover Mordred's retreat. Of brave Sir Bors, who tried to rally the knights as the grey light returned. But the heart had gone out of them all when Arthur died, and they'd barely managed to get the king's body off the battlefield before the Saxon barbarians got hold of it.

Soon everyone in the hall was weeping, except for Rhianna. She kept her back very straight, still seeing Mordred's axe come down on the king's head. Any tears were frozen inside her. She felt only hatred for the dark knight who had killed her father.

Then Merlin's song changed. The violence of the battle faded from the walls, and people smiled in relief as silver bathed the crystal once more.

"Four Lights stand against the dark," the druid sang, and a strange unearthly music filled the hall. "The Sword Excalibur, that was forged in Avalon…"

A gleaming sword shimmered in the walls, the white jewel on its hilt shining moon-bright.

"The Lance of Truth made by the hands of men…"

A knight's long jousting lance replaced the sword. A green ribbon fluttered from its shaft.

"The Crown of Dreams, which hides the jewel of Annwn…"

The lance gave way to a glittering crown set with fiery gemstones.

"And the Grail said to hold all the stars in heaven."

As the crown faded, Rhianna held her breath, remembering her strange dream in the wood. But no image of the Grail appeared in the crystal walls. Only the stars shone through from the wood, a little brighter than before.

A great sigh rippled round the hall as Merlin put his gnarled hand across the harp strings to silence them.

"I'd no idea that fool Bors meant to throw the sword into the lake," he said, "or I'd have taken it off him. But what's done is done. Now it has been returned to the Lady of the Lake, she will keep it until one of the Pendragon blood comes to claim it. If Rhianna can recover Excalibur and bring it back to Avalon, that should keep the Sword out of Mordred's hands, at least, and give

Arthur the strength to finish him once he wakes. The dark knight may yet find a way to get the Crown from the dragon, but the Lance was broken years ago, and it's anyone's guess where the Grail is now, so we should have a fair chance of defeating him if it comes to a battle. I still say it's no task for a girl, but the alternative is unthinkable… If Mordred ever gets his hands on all four Lights, both our worlds will fall into the dark, and the heroes in our caverns will sleep for ever, their souls lost to Annwn for all time. Do you accept this quest, Rhianna Pendragon?"

A cloud drifted across the stars. A few people sniffed and wiped their eyes. Everyone stared at Rhianna as she stood. She felt glad of the long skirt that hid her shaking knees.

"Of course I do!" she said, her voice ringing across the hall. "If the sword will help my father defeat Mordred, then I have to find it as soon as possible." She felt a bit relieved she wouldn't actually be expected to fight the dark knight herself. "When do we start?"

Another sigh passed around the room. One by one, the Avalonians touched their hands to their foreheads in respect and murmured "*Faha'ruh*", the way they did to their own Lord Avallach. Even the boys who had teased her earlier smiled at her and wished her luck. More used to being made fun of, Rhianna flushed.

Merlin set down the harp, suddenly looking very tired. "Naturally I will help the girl as much as I can, and Prince Elphin will accompany her to represent Avalon. Arthur's knights are waiting, so we'd best get going as soon as it's light. Any questions?"

Nobody spoke. Elphin's mother held out her

arms to her son. Rhianna felt a bit left out when the Lady of Avalon hugged him. Then she remembered she had a mother of her own in the human world. Very soon now, if all went well, she would be meeting her.

"I have a question!" Rhianna said. "What if Mordred finds Excalibur first? Do I have to look for these other Light things as well? The, er, crown and such?" She thought uneasily of the dragon in Merlin's song-pictures.

The gathering whispered in concern. Someone mentioned the Wild Hunt, and was hastily shushed.

Merlin frowned at her. "No point worrying our heads about that unless we have to. By all accounts Mordred's in no fit state to go swimming at the moment. We'll have the advantage."

Rhianna smiled, looking forward to swimming in the waters of another world. "How long have I got before my father wakes up and needs his sword?" she asked, anxious to be back before then.

"Long enough. Arthur will be reborn when the time is right," Merlin said in his annoyingly cryptic way. "The important thing is to stop Mordred getting hold of the Lights and using them for his own ends in the meantime."

Rhianna wondered if she dared demand they allow her into the crystal caverns to see the king's body before she went. But such a visit would only delay them… After hearing Merlin's song of dragons and battles, she wanted to get going as soon as possible.

"Is my mother still alive?" she blurted out. "Does she know about me?"

She had a hundred other questions. But the druid rose stiffly from his stool and took her elbow. He steered her firmly across to the royal couches. "Later, Rhianna," he said. "Yes, the queen lives, and she knows you were taken to Avalon to keep you safe. If I start to explain everything now, we'll be here all winter. There'll be plenty of time to answer your questions when we reach the world of men."

"That's another thing," Rhianna said. "How do we get to my father's world? Do we have to go through the mists in your little boat? Because it looks too small for all of us and the horses as well, and Elphin's scared of wa—" She caught the look on her friend's face and changed what she was going to say. "Elphin can't swim," she finished.

Merlin chuckled. She glared at him.

Would the druid laugh if *his* father's body lay in the crystal caverns awaiting rebirth?

"Put the poor girl out of her misery, Avallach!" Elphin's mother said. "She thinks you're going to make her leave her beloved Alba behind. Our Elphin looks a bit green round the ears, too."

Lord Avallach smiled at them. "Don't worry, my children. Do you think the Wild Hunt uses little boats? We'll shoe your horses with silver tonight, and tomorrow they will carry you so swiftly over the water you'll hardly realise it's there. Merlin will follow you in his boat, since I can never tempt him on to one of our mist horses. Now, I suggest you both get some sleep. Tomorrow is going to be a long day."

◀ 3 ▶

Through
the Mist

So brave Rhianna crossed water wide
With the Prince of Avalon at her side,
On horses born of mist and myth
Shod in silver by a six-fingered smith.

At dawn, Rhianna and Elphin held their
horses at the water's edge while Lord
Avallach gave them last-moment instructions.
Her friend listened carefully, but Rhianna

barely heard a word. She'd dreamed of this day for so long, she could hardly believe it was happening. Before the sun set, they'd be on the other side of the mists in the land of men! Little shivers of excitement kept running through her. Merlin had promised that Arthur's knights would be waiting for them, and she could already imagine the ranks of warriors on their great horses with their colourful banners snapping in the wind of another world. Maybe her mother would even be waiting with them?

Over on the jetty, Merlin shipped his oars and checked his cargo. As well as several sacks of sweet apples, he had jars of healing herbs that grew only in Avalon, so he was taking a good supply. Elphin's mother had put together a picnic for their journey, which had to go in the boat, too. Merlin also had their packs of spare clothes, though Rhianna had insisted on carrying her father's shield and wearing her new armour. Elphin had his precious harp in a deerskin bag.

Finally, Lord Avallach hugged them both, and they trotted their horses into the shallows. But their legs did not dissolve into mist on touching the water, as usually happened. Instead, Alba's silver-shod hooves pranced lightly over the surface, sending up a glittering spray. *This is fun*, said the mare. Elphin clutched his harp close to his chest, eyeing the water warily.

Rhianna laughed at his expression. "Just don't drop it," she said.

Soon the enchanted mist curled around them, and the shore faded from sight until it seemed they rode in the middle of a cloud. She longed to let Alba gallop. But Merlin rowed steadily, his oars plopping like little fish. They did not head straight across as Rhianna had imagined. Instead, they set off in a loop around the island with Merlin leading the way, the silver spiral on his staff shining like a star in the bows. The mist grew thicker and began to sparkle, and she smelled magic. She glanced back to check on Elphin. He gave her a small, worried smile. When she turned round again, Merlin and his boat had disappeared.

Unease crept over her as she realised she'd lost all sense of direction. What if they got lost out here and never found the shore again? Then she saw a shadow off to her left, blurred by enchantments. "There he is!" Not waiting for Elphin, she urged Alba into a canter to catch up.

"Rhia!" Elphin called from a long way off. "Wait…"

It wasn't Merlin's boat. Rhianna pulled Alba to a snorting stop. Squinting at the shadow, she thought she saw the druid standing on a rock with his staff raised to make purple lightning. A sudden chill seized her. Her skin prickled as something large and dark flapped past. The light dimmed still further, and for a horrible moment she was alone in the mists between worlds with unseen wings beating overhead. Dizzy, she gripped Alba's mane and peered nervously at the sky. What if the mare misted, and she fell off out here? Then she heard Evenstar's hooves splashing behind her and the light returned, showing them the shoreline through the thinning haze.

Is it another race? Alba asked flattening her ears at the other horse. Spooked by what she'd seen in the mist, Rhianna gladly loosened the reins to let the mare have her head. Merlin could look after himself, she decided, laughing in relief as the spray soaked her cheeks. It was like galloping through diamonds. Her heavy braid bounced on the shield strapped to her back. Alba's silver-shod hooves flew over the water, carrying her towards her father's land. Thinking of the dark wings, she let the mare gallop faster and further than she should have. Only when the horse's hooves struck gravel did she reluctantly rein Alba back to a trot and look round for her friend.

Elphin pulled up on her tail, breathing hard. "Are you all right?" he said. "That was a strong enchantment – I thought I'd lost you back there! Are those King Arthur's knights, do you think?"

Rhianna gave the beach a second look. She'd thought it deserted. But now she saw a small band of men wearing dirty red cloaks, huddled under some willows that had already lost half their leaves. This beach had stones rather than sand, and the mist curling over the water was grey with rain rather than silver and luminous. An island with a single black hill rose out of the marshes nearby, and she could just make out a cluster of huts on its shore. There was no sign of the colourful army of knights she'd been expecting. And it was *cold*.

She pulled her cloak closer in disappointment. "Must be, I suppose."

"Where's Merlin?"

"I don't know. I didn't see where he went." That shadow she'd seen in the mist... if it hadn't been Merlin, what else had it been?

"Maybe we should wait for him before we show ourselves?" Elphin said.

But then one of the horses on the beach whinnied, and both Avalonian horses pricked their ears and whinnied back. "Too late," Rhianna said as the men shouted and pointed at them. "Come on, let's get out of this mist. We didn't pass the boat, so maybe he's already landed."

"Be careful, Rhia. Remember they're at war here—"

His warning fell on deaf ears. Even though this wasn't quite the welcome she'd imagined, excitement filled her as Alba splashed out of the shallows. As they trotted up the beach towards the waiting men, she slipped the dragon shield over her arm, doing up the straps with her teeth. She tossed her cloak back over her shoulder so her Avalonian armour glimmered silver in the rain. "Look graceful, Alba," she muttered.

I am always graceful, the mare replied, arching her neck. *That is a fine stallion!*

The knights stiffened, and the biggest one stepped forward and drew his sword. Behind him, a round-faced boy with a mop of straw-coloured hair struggled to hold a large bay horse that danced at the ends of its reins, whinnying to Alba. There were only four of them, Rhianna saw now – the big knight, the boy, and two other knights who held their own horses. But they were all armed. One man had a lance as well as a sword. Even the boy had a little dagger stuck through his tight belt. She could see no sign of Merlin. Suddenly, Elphin's warning made sense. Not that she could do much about it now.

"Are you King Arthur's men?" she asked, bringing Alba to a prancing halt.

The big knight stared at her. He had a curly brown beard and smelled as if he hadn't washed lately. Warily, he lowered his sword and peered closer at the shield she carried. He blinked in surprise. "That's the king's shield!" After the Avalonian songs, his voice sounded gruff to her ears. "Where did you find it, damsel?"

"Merlin gave it to me, of course," Rhianna said. "He'll be here soon, I expect. I'm Rhianna. We got separated in the mist. He's a bit slow, I'm afraid. He's bringing the boat with our luggage." She turned in her saddle to see where Elphin had got to.

The knight raised his sword again as Elphin joined them. "What you got in the bag, son?" he demanded, his tone suddenly hard.

"Only my harp," Elphin answered. Lifting it out, he began to strum gently. The Avalonian music tinkled in the rain, making the other knights smile.

The plump boy's eyes widened as he noticed Elphin's extra fingers. "He's one of *them*, sir!"

"I can see that." The curly-haired knight narrowed his eyes at her friend and peered at the water. "I see two fairy horses of the enchanted isle. But I don't see no boat. How do I know you didn't just steal the king's shield? What did you say your name was, damsel?"

"Rhianna Pendragon! And this is my friend Prince Elphin from Avalon. We've come to find my father's sword, Excalibur. Merlin says some idiot knight threw it into a lake, so I expect I've got to swim down and fetch it out again. I don't suppose you know where it is, do you?"

The boy's eyes widened even further as she spoke. The other two knights led their horses closer, looking up at her face. One had fair hair and a fresh sword cut on his cheek and looked quite young. The other was tall and thin with black hair and a scowl.

"Could be her, Bors," said the young one, smiling at Rhianna. "She has the queen's colouring, same freckles on her nose even. And she must have met Merlin, if she knows about Excalibur."

"Bit of a wild look about her, but that's probably from growing up on the enchanted isle," grunted the dark-haired knight. "Don't expect they've got much in the way of courtly manners over there. She might scrub up once we get to Camelot, and the other girls teach her what a hairbrush is."

The boy giggled, and Rhianna flushed.

"I can brush my hair later! Right now we've

got work to do, before Mordred realises I'm here. Also, where I come from it's polite to introduce yourselves. So your name's Bors…?" Her voice trailed off as she realised her big mouth had got her into trouble again. *That fool Sir Bors.*

To her surprise the big knight laughed, a deep laugh from the belly. "Yup, I'm Sir Bors. The idiot who threw Arthur's sword into the lake, at your service, my lady!" He swept her a mocking bow. "Someone had to carry out the king's dying wish. The grumpy one who doesn't know how to smile is Sir Agravaine. Sir Bedivere's the handsome one who couldn't bring himself to throw Excalibur away when the king ordered him to. And the lad swallowing flies back there is my squire, Cai, named after King Arthur's brother may

God rest his soul… Close your mouth, Cai, before some of young Elphin's magic flies in and turns you into a frog."

Cai gulped and stared warily at the shimmering harp. Elphin smiled and slipped it back into his bag so it wouldn't get any wetter. He winked at Rhianna, and she knew his music had contained magic to lift the men's mood.

"So now we're all introduced, and I suppose we can assume you are who you claim to be," continued Sir Bors. "No other damsel's likely to be riding around these marshes on a fairy horse carrying Arthur's shield, at any rate. Merlin told us he was going to fetch Arthur's daughter when he took the king's body across, though he didn't say nothing about your companion… but that's Merlin for you. 'Wait here' he says, as if we've got nothing better to do than hang about the marshes all night! I'll admit it was a bit of a surprise to learn you was hidden away in Avalon all this time, but Merlin does love his little secrets. And I always said that business with the queen's kidnapping when she was pregnant with you was a bit convenient, like."

The knight scratched his head and squinted out into the mist. "Well, no point us all standing about out here getting soaked! Merlin's probably got some druid business over on the Tor that's delayed him. Let's rig a shelter in the trees and wait for him. Cai, stop swinging off them reins and go see if you can find us some dry wood."

As Sir Bors took his horse from the relieved boy, Rhianna peered into the mist as well, thinking uneasily of the winged shadow she'd seen. She frowned and patted poor Alba.

The mare was shivering in the rain. A shelter and fire sounded a very good idea. In this weather, she wouldn't need all those flimsy dresses Elphin's mother had helped her pack, anyway.

❦

Night fell quickly in the world of men. The rain eventually stopped, but the trees still dripped. Rhianna and Elphin huddled miserably under the shelter with Cai, while Sir Bors and the other knights tried to light a fire with the damp wood the boy had collected. They weren't having much success. Their idea of supper proved to be stale bread and tough, salty strips of what looked like leather, but which Cai claimed was meat. Rhianna discovered she'd lost her appetite. She offered her bread to Alba, who chewed it half-heartedly.

Not as nice as apples, the mare decided.

"Are you really from Avalon?" Cai asked, gulping down his share as if it might be his last meal ever. "I heard if humans eat there, they can't come back again. But Merlin usually does when he goes there – though he's only half human, of course, even if he can do magic and stuff. Wish he was here now. He'd have our fire going in no time… Are you going to eat that?" Having finished his own share, he eyed Rhianna's meat.

She passed it to him, and he tore at it hungrily with strong teeth.

Elphin hadn't even touched his. He watched the boy with a disgusted expression. "Don't you have any decent food here?"

"Not good enough for you, your highness?" Cai scowled. "You're lucky, you've got half my ration. So what do you eat in Avalon?"

Elphin smiled. "We eat wild strawberries with Avalonian honey, mushrooms flavoured with unicorn horn, and... cakes made with flour ground from human bones," he teased.

Cai eyed him sideways. "Really? What do the cakes taste like?"

"Pretty good, actually. Especially when Mother makes them with the bones of plump human squires Father brings back from the Hunt."

Cai paled. "Well, you'd better go back to Avalon then, because we don't make cakes out of human bones here. Even the Saxons wouldn't do that."

"Oh stop it, you two!" Rhianna said, slapping away an insect. "Don't listen to him, Cai. The Hunt doesn't bring back bodies, only souls, and you can't make cakes out of souls. We're wasting time. We should be going to find Excalibur, not waiting around here for Merlin, getting cold and wet and bitten. Where *is* he, the old fool?" But she felt bad because she knew it was her fault they'd lost him. She wondered what they would do if he didn't turn up.

Elphin glanced at her as he reached for his harp. "Shall I play something to make us warmer? I might be able to light our fire if I try."

"No," Cai said quickly. "Someone might hear you." He glanced nervously at the trees.

"Someone like your evil Prince Mordred, you mean?" Elphin asked. "I saw him in Merlin's song-pictures. He looked very violent."

"What's a song-picture?" Cai asked with his mouth full. "And did Mordred look very ugly? He left Camelot before I joined the squire school, thank God. He used to be quite handsome, but apparently he got cut up bad in the battle – serves him right for killing King Arthur, that's what I say! But then Merlin took the king's body into the mists... Is it true people don't die in Avalon?"

Rhianna shook away an image of Mordred's axe coming down on her father's head. "Sort of," she said, thinking of the king's body in the crystal caverns. They could be here all night explaining Avalon's magic to the boy. She still had a hundred questions of her own. "What did Sir Bors mean about the queen being kidnapped? He means my mother, doesn't he? How did it happen?"

Cai frowned. "Dunno. I weren't born back then, though the older squires still talk about it sometimes. Some upstart lord was supposed to have carried her off one night and imprisoned her on the Lonely Tor right over there." He pointed to the hill, black against the stars. "She vanished so completely, some people say she was stolen away by the fairies... sorry, no offence." He glanced warily at Elphin's harp. "But King Arthur led some of his knights to rescue her, attacked the Tor by moonlight and galloped back across the water with Queen Guinevere in his arms. Merlin parted the sea for him – that must have been something to see! I bet that stupid lord who kidnapped her got a shock. Afterwards the queen founded that monastery over there, so anyone else who got stuck on the island would have a safe place to go. I bet that's where Merlin's sleeping tonight."

Rhianna eyed the cluster of huts, barely visible in the dark. If the druid was sleeping in a warm bed tonight while they camped out here in the rain, she'd have something to say to him in the morning.

"We don't take humans to Avalon against their will," Elphin said, frowning.

Except when they're babies and can't protest, Rhianna thought. When Cai opened his mouth to ask yet another question, she got in first. "When King Arthur got the queen back, was she still pregnant?" she asked.

"Oh, no! That's the whole point!" Cai finished the last crumbs and grinned. "Her baby was gone. Everyone thought she'd lost it with all the upset. But now here you are, come out of the mists… I reckon them people who say she was kidnapped by the fairy lord were right. What was it like growing up in Avalon? Is Lord Avallach as terrible as they say?"

Rhianna glanced at Elphin. *Fairy*. She hadn't

heard the word before today. Judging by the way his eyes had turned purple it must be an insult. Remembering all the teasing she'd endured in Avalon for not having any magic, she felt a sudden sympathy for her friend. Here Elphin would get teased, because he was the different one in this world. She wanted to say something nice about his people. But before she could tell Cai how kind and generous Lord Avallach had been to her, and how he had given her Alba and her beautiful armour, Elphin touched her arm. He was staring into the darkness.

"Something's out there," he whispered.

Sir Bors whirled, his hand dropping to his sword hilt. Sir Bedivere and Sir Agravaine were still arguing over how best to light the fire. "Quiet!" Bors hissed. "Might be Saxons." He put a finger to his lips and pointed at the trees. The three knights crept warily into the shadows, their swords drawn.

Rhianna held her breath. She hadn't heard anything. But Elphin's ears were sharper than human ears.

"Is it Merlin?" she whispered back.

"I don't think so," he said, his hand creeping towards his harp.

Cai moaned. "I feel sick."

"Serves you right for eating so much," Rhianna said.

"Shh!" Elphin breathed. "There's something very dark out there, I can't—"

A grunt came from the trees, and Sir Agravaine shouted, "Got him!"

Sir Bors raced after his friend, and the wood erupted with thuds and yells and the clash of swords.

Leaves showered their shelter as something heavy crashed down upon it. Cai yelled and fumbled for his knife. Elphin covered his harp with his body. Rhianna grabbed the dragon shield and dived for the disappearing gap. She could see Alba tugging at her tether and whinnying in terror and Elphin's little Evenstar rearing. Then the shelter collapsed on her legs, and she sprawled face down in the mud.

She just had time to raise the shield over her head as a huge, black-winged creature dived out of the night towards her, trailing blue mist. It hit the shield with a thud, and cold rippled up her arm. Something dark and terrifying flickered inside her head. "I SEE YOU, PENDRAGON," it roared.

Then it was gone.

Merlin Makes
a Mistake

Mordred watched in his mirror as the dragon flapped away across the water, its wings trailing blue mist. So much for his mother's magic – she'd promised him the creature would disable the girl until his men could get there, yet it had been turned aside by the Pendragon's old shield! He hadn't even got a proper look at his cousin. Pathetic. Where was his mother, anyway?

He peered deeper into the glass. At first all he could see was the cursed mist, sparkling with enchantments. Then he saw a lone hill with a black tower on the top. It looked a bit like the island where his Aunt Guinevere had founded some kind of village for priests of the Christ-god, only different somehow. Thunder rumbled around the hill. In its shadow a small boat floated upside down. An oar drifted between the rocks, blackened and splintered, with what looked like a bundle of rags clinging to it. As the dark wings passed overhead, the rags stirred and a knobbly hand flicked a weak enchantment into the air.

"Merlin!" Mordred breathed, drawing back a bit from the mirror in case the interfering old druid could see him.

The dragon gave a shriek, swooped down and snatched something silver from the water. Lightning flickered, showing this to be the spiral charm from the end of Merlin's staff.

Before Mordred could see any more, a ragged hole appeared in the storm clouds and swallowed the creature.

For a moment he thought Merlin had tricked them. Then black mist swirled on the beach and took the form of his mother cloaked in shadows. She held what remained of the druid's staff with its end thrust towards the drowning man.

"Take hold, Merlin!" she called in her sweetest voice. "I'll pull you ashore."

Mordred grinned. This should be entertaining.

The druid raised his head and squinted at the beach, as if he couldn't quite see who had spoken. He probably couldn't. If Mordred knew his mother at all, she had enchanted herself to appear as somebody else.

But he had underestimated Merlin, as usual.

"Where is she, witch?" he croaked. "If you've hurt her—"

"Why worry about a silly girl who just wants to gallop about on horseback?" The witch's voice became soft and persuasive. "You're too old for this, Merlin. You could barely fight off that shadrake, could you? You had quite enough trouble with Arthur. His daughter's a lost cause believe me. You'll drown if you stay out there much longer. Let me help you. Take hold!"

Merlin eyed the staff. Mordred could almost see the old druid's thoughts working: without it, he would be helpless against his enemy's dark magic. With visible effort, he reached out a trembling hand and closed his fingers about the splintered end.

The witch gave a shout of triumph, and the staff turned into a ghostly green snake that whipped its dark coils about the druid's wrist and bit him. Poison filled his body, immobilising him. Then the snake dragged him underwater. A stream of bubbles rose to the surface, a glimmering thread floated out of the water and into the mist, and all was calm.

Back on the beach, Mordred's mother dusted off her hands and laughed. "You can't help them now, old fool!" she called. "Bringing the girl out of Avalon was your biggest mistake yet. She won't survive the winter."

Mordred chuckled too, and his mother whirled to face him, fingers pointed in the witch-sign. When she saw him flinch, she lowered her hand and smiled. "Oh, it's you, Mordred. Spying on me, I see! At least you're learning to use that mirror I gave you. Well, my son? Did you like what you saw?"

"Is Merlin dead?" Mordred asked, curious about that glimmer he'd seen.

"Dead enough. His body is useless to him now, and he's the last of his kind. I doubt he can manage the spirit transfer on his own – but even if he does, he'll be of little threat to us without his druid's staff."

"Your creature failed," Mordred said sulkily. "The girl's still free."

"I can't do everything for you. Get those lazy blood-drinkers of yours after her! They should find it easy enough now the druid's out of the way. I'm dead, remember? There's a limit to my powers in your world." As she spoke, her cloak dissolved once more into black mist and the mirror showed him his own face.

Mordred scowled at the sword cut on his cheek. His body wasn't healing fast enough. His men were looking for Excalibur. They knew nothing yet about Arthur's daughter. It might take them all winter to find the sword and report back to him, and by that time his cousin could be anywhere. She might even flee back to Avalon after the shadrake's attack. Most damsels he knew would have fainted at the very sight of the creature. Why on earth hadn't his mother snatched *her* instead of Merlin as they came through the mists?

But at least the girl didn't have the druid to look after her any more. His mother was right. It would be like hunting baby rabbits with his favourite hawk. Mordred smiled, feeling a bit better. He'd always enjoyed hearing their helpless squeals.

◄ 4 ►

The Road
to Camelot

Through the Summer Lands they rode all day
  And along many a broad Roman way,
To Camelot where King Arthur was crowned
  By his finest knights at a table round.

Warily, Rhianna lifted the edge of the shield and peered out into the night. Strange lights flickered over the marsh and a rotten smell hung in the air. For a heartbeat she saw a black tower on the crest of the Tor, silhouetted against purple storm clouds and with black wings flapping around it. Then the lights faded and the tower vanished.

Alba whinnied to her. *I need help.*

She picked herself up and hurried to the mare, whose lead rope had become tangled with those of the other horses. By the time she had sorted them out and soothed the trembling mist horses, Elphin and Cai had emerged from beneath the collapsed shelter and the knights had stopped fighting.

"Geroff me, you great oafs!" Sir Bedivere spluttered.

Shamefaced, Sir Agravaine and Sir Bors sheathed their swords and let their friend get up out of the mud. There had been no enemy in the trees, after all. In their confusion and the shadows, they had been fighting each other.

Sir Bedivere retrieved his sword, wiped wet leaves from the blade and glared at them. "What were you trying to do? Are you blind, or something?"

"You nearly took my hand off," Sir Agravaine said.

"Well, what do you expect? Jumping me out of the dark like that... you should watch it. I might have killed you."

"Ha! That'll be the day. Soft Hands Bedivere, killing somebody."

"That's enough, you two," Sir Bors snapped. "You're forgetting our charges. Are you all right, Princess Rhianna?"

Rhianna didn't feel much like a princess with soggy leaves all down her front and mud on her face. She almost giggled. Then she remembered Lord Avallach's warning about Mordred hunting her, and the smile died on her lips. She nodded. "I'm fine."

"What *was* that thing?" Cai stared at their fallen shelter. The canvas glittered with ice crystals and bore the marks of large claws.

"A dragon?" Sir Bedivere suggested. "Like the one that stole Arthur's crown?"

Sir Bors frowned into the mist, paling now with the dawn. "There ain't supposed to be no dragons left in these parts. Looked like it came over from the Tor, which is bad news if that's where Merlin went."

Elphin glanced up from checking his harp. "I think it was a shadrake from Annwn," he said quietly. "They're supposed to be related to dragons, except they breathe ice instead of fire. I've never seen one before, but the mists between worlds are thin here... it must have slipped through when Merlin opened the way."

Rhianna turned cold all over. Annwn... the land of shadow, where the Wild Hunt took the souls of the dead that had nowhere else to go. She could only imagine what horrors might live there, because whenever the Avalonians sang about Annwn, the crystal walls of Lord Avallach's palace turned black.

The knights glanced uneasily at one another. Cai made the sign of a cross over his chest. Rhianna wondered what it meant, but was more worried about how they were going to find Excalibur without Merlin's help.

"Right," Sir Bors broke the frightened silence. "It obviously ain't safe for us to stay here. We can't wait for Merlin no longer. I vote we escort Damsel Rhianna and her fairy friend to Camelot, where we can at least protect them properly while we decide what to do next. Merlin's bound to realise we've gone there, and if he don't turn up we can always try using the Round Table to contact him, like Arthur used to do when he was off on his druid business."

"I don't need protecting…" Rhianna began, but closed her mouth when she caught Elphin's warning glance. His eyes were deep purple with agitation.

"Just wait till you see King Arthur's famous table!" Cai said, brightening. "There's none like it in the whole world. It almost fills the Great Hall, which is bigger than anybody else's. Then there's the jousting court, where we—"

"Cai," Sir Bors growled. "Save it for later and go saddle my horse."

It did not take them long to pack. Their shelter was down already, and their unlit fire didn't need putting out. All they had to do was load up their luggage. Sir Bors mounted his big bay horse and took the lead; Sir Agravaine, carrying the lance, brought up the rear on his black stallion, while Sir Bedivere took Cai on the hindquarters of his chestnut. The plump boy didn't look very comfortable and clung to Sir Bedivere's waist. Rhianna rode knee to knee with Elphin, the two mist horses looking very small and delicate beside the knights' big warhorses. She kept her shield on her arm and eyed the marshes warily as Sir Bors led them along narrow, raised tracks that seemed to vanish into the mist behind them.

"Could that dragon-creature have had something to do with Merlin's disappearance, do you think?" she whispered to her friend as they went.

"I hope not," Elphin said. "But dragons collect treasure to build their nests and I don't suppose shadrakes are much different, so it could have been attracted to his staff shining in the mists. It's a good thing you haven't got Excalibur yet, or it might not have given up so easily." His fingers clutched at the bag containing his harp. He looked pale.

"What's wrong?" Rhianna asked.

He said tightly, "I tried to use my magic to help you, but it didn't work properly. When I saw that thing dive at you, I thought... I thought it was going to kill you!" His eyes had gone such a deep purple they appeared black.

"Oh, stop it," Rhianna said, embarrassed. "That creature came out of nowhere. You hardly had much chance to get out your harp and start singing, did you? Anyway, I had my shield, so it didn't hurt me."

Elphin frowned. "But it could have done! You're only human."

Rhianna had to laugh. She slapped his knee playfully. "Cheer up, Elphin. It's not so bad being human, you know. I'm used to it."

"But Father said I had to—"

"Protect me. I know." She grinned again. "But I already told Sir Bors, I don't need protecting. Just wait till we find my father's sword. Then I'll be the one protecting you!"

My father was king of this land, she reminded herself firmly, which made it her land too. There was nothing to fear while his knights rode with them.

She sat straighter in her saddle and stared

around curiously as the countryside unfolded before them. As they rode out of the marshes on to drier ground, the mists rolled back and the sun shone through, turning the trees around them to a blaze of gold. They cantered on springy green turf along a wide straight track, a bit overgrown in places but good for the horses. With the blue skies and fresh autumn breeze, her spirits soon lifted.

They passed an empty villa with a red roof, its whitewashed walls covered with ivy. Coloured tiles showed through the weeds in the courtyard. She wanted to stop and look at the pattern, but Bors had already trotted past. When she asked the other two knights who had lived there, Sir Agravaine muttered "Romans" under his breath and refused to say any more.

Then they came to a town, where half the houses were burned-out shells. People ran out when they heard the horses' hooves, and called after the knights to send help. Small children with grubby faces clung to the women's skirts, staring wide-eyed at the two mist horses.

Sir Bors pressed his lips together and led them quickly past. "Saxons have been this way," he said. "We're too noticeable with them fairy horses. I'd leave them behind, if it wouldn't slow us down too much. Keep your eyes peeled."

Please do not leave me here, said Alba.

"Of course we won't leave you, silly," Rhianna said, scowling at the big knight. Just let him try to make her.

She felt relieved when they left the town behind. Her neck prickled and she kept turning her head, imagining dark wings following them.

She couldn't stop thinking about that hiss she'd heard in her head. *I see you, Pendragon.* Was it Mordred's creature? Well, she'd be ready for it next time.

More wary of Saxons than dragons, Sir Bors and Sir Agravaine rode with their hands on their swords, while Sir Bedivere told Cai to be ready with his dagger in case of trouble. Elphin loosened the strings of his harp bag and kept a wary lookout with his violet eyes. Rhianna wished she had Excalibur, and wondered why her father had told his knights to throw the magic sword away if he'd know it gave him strength.

When the sun set, they rode off the road and up a hill, where they made camp inside a circle of stones marked with curious lines and spirals.

Cai gathered wood, and this time Elphin breathed a long, low note over the fire and the spark from Sir Bors' flint caught straight away.

Cai stared at the Avalonian boy, impressed. "That's nearly as good as Merlin does it!" he said. "Can you do any other magic?"

"Don't take much magic to light dry wood and sheep's wool," Bors muttered, scowling at the squire. "Leave him be, Cai. This ain't the place for silly tricks."

But as they shared out the last of the stale bread Elphin looked much happier than he had that morning. This time Rhianna was hungry enough to eat her ration, though she kept the crust for Alba. "I promise I'll get you a whole bucket of apples when we reach Camelot," she told the mare as she fed the bread to her. Although the rain had stopped and the stars glittered like they did in Avalon, the night was chilly. She pulled her cloak around her and stared out into the darkness beyond the glow of their fire, wondering if she would always feel this cold in her father's world.

Elphin came to join her and rested a hand on one of the tall stones. His fingers traced the spirals. "There's power in these," he said. "Faint, but I can feel it… echoes of men's songs."

"Your magic still works, doesn't it?" Rhianna said.

"Yes – in this place, anyway."

"Good. Do you know how to get us back to Avalon?"

Elphin eyed her sideways. "Had enough of the world of men already?"

"Of course not! I just mean if we find Excalibur, and Merlin doesn't turn up in time."

Her friend pulled a face. "I don't know, Rhia. Even Merlin said he found the way through the mists difficult last time, didn't he?"

"But you're Lord Avallach's son. You *must* know how to get home."

"I'm not old enough to lead the Wild Hunt yet."

"What's that got to do with it? Can't you use your harp somehow?"

"Sorry, Rhia… all I know is Merlin wasn't meant to get lost."

Rhianna sighed. "I suppose we'll have to find him, then." She'd been hoping they could complete their quest without the grumpy old druid and show him she could handle a magic sword as well as any son of Arthur's would have done.

Elphin gave her a sharp look. "You're

shivering," he said, suddenly concerned. "Let's go back to the fire. I didn't help light it so that lump Cai could hog it all night."

Rhianna giggled. "Shh! He's listening."

"He's still a lump. I've never seen anyone eat so fast, have you?" Elphin raised his voice. "Better slow down, human squire, or Sir Bedivere's poor horse will collapse under your weight!"

Cai laughed. "You'd eat fast, too, fairy boy, if the Saxons kept stealing all your food!" he called back. "Not all of us can magic apples out of thin air, you know. Besides, you've never been in the squires' dining hall at the end of a long day running around after the knights in the jousting court. You'll find out!"

Rhianna had never seen Elphin magic an apple out of the air, either. But she was glad to return to the warmth of the fire. While the three knights patrolled the stones with their hands on their swords, she rested her head on her father's shield and stared up at the stars. "What's Camelot like?" she asked.

"Huge!" Cai said. "It stands up on great hill, all shining white like the moon. It's got ramparts all around, and the deepest ditches and the tallest towers in the world, and no Saxon has ever set foot inside its gates and lived to tell the tale. There's room inside the walls for all of King Arthur's knights and their horses and families and hawks and everything else. There's a school for us squires training to be knights, and the Damsel Tower for the girls, and a chapel for the Christ-god and his priests. The Great Hall has a mosaic on the floor better than any you'll find in Rome, and in the middle is the Round Table which Merlin enchanted, so there would always be enough seats for all the knights who want to sit with the king. And because it's round, none of them sit higher than any of the others, so whatever they discuss is fair and equal, and no knight can break a promise he makes when he sits there... least they couldn't until that idiot Mordred killed the king." He paused for breath. "I'm sorry, Damsel Rhianna, I forgot. It must be sad for you to hear about King Arthur's death, with him being your father and all."

"It's all right," she said, eager to find out as much as possible about her parents' home. "Does the queen sit at the Round Table as well?"

"I dunno," Cai said. "I never went in there when they discussed stuff – squires aren't allowed to sit at the table till they get knighted. But now King Arthur's dead and gone for ever,

I suppose no one will get knighted. Least not till we get another king at Camelot…"

"King Arthur's not gone for ever," Elphin corrected. "His body's in Avalon, awaiting rebirth."

"Really?" Cai looked interested. "Then you mean he's goin' to come back and save us from the Saxons and Prince Mordred, after all?"

"He might after I take him Excalibur," Rhianna said.

Cai gave her an alarmed look. "I'd stay away from that sword if I were you, Damsel Rhianna! It feeds on people's souls."

"How?" Rhianna said, chilled. Maybe it had tried to swallow her father's soul, and that was why he had ordered it thrown away?

But Cai wasn't much help. He shrugged. "Magic, of course." He turned back to Elphin, his eyes shining. "So King Arthur's in Lord Avallach's palace? Just wait till I tell the other squires! Wonder what he'll think of the place when he wakes up. I bet it isn't half as grand as Camelot."

"Does Camelot have walls of crystal that can show song-pictures, and enchanted caverns that keep people alive for ever?" Elphin said.

"We got dungeons," Cai said, not to be outdone. "Though people don't usually live too long down there."

Soon the two boys were deep in an argument as to which world had the best royal building. When Elphin got out his harp and began to strum gently, Rhianna closed her eyes with a smile and let the music drift over her. Cai didn't stand a chance.

She fell asleep thinking of her father's body lying in Merlin's boat and had the strangest dream.

The old druid limped up the hill towards the stone circle, stabbing his staff into the grass. He had the same bedraggled falcon's feathers in his beard as the day he'd brought King Arthur to Avalon.

As he stepped between the stones, a fierce note made Rhianna's ears ring, and there was a flash of silver light. She flinched as the druid turned his pale blue gaze upon her.

"Ah, there you are, Rhianna Pendragon!" he said in his grumpy manner. "I thought you might camp here. If you are dreaming this, something has gone wrong. Take the sword to Camelot and wait for me there. Do not try to use it! Do you hear? I will come to you as soon as I can. If all else fails, I'll send you my pathfinder…" His image wavered and blurred like a song-picture. "Look for the dragon… spirit transfer… beware Mordred."

Her tongue unlocked. "Merlin! What dragon? Do you mean the shadrake that attacked us at the Tor? What's a spirit transfer? I haven't got Excalibur yet. Where are you? How do we find the lake? We need you—"

But there was another flash of light, and the druid vanished. Elphin had stopped playing, and the rest of her dreams were a confusion of black wings and swirling mist.

A big hand shook her awake. "Damsel Rhianna?" Sir Bors said gruffly. "It's dawn. We should get going now."

It began to rain again as they rejoined the Roman road, a fine drizzle that found its way into every gap of their clothing and hid their surroundings. Evenstar misted to avoid the worst of it, making Sir Agravaine, who rode at the back, blink and rub his eyes. Alba bent her head to her chest. *Water is getting in my ears*, the mare sulked. *I want to mist as well.*

"Don't you dare," Rhianna muttered. "If you make me fall off here, I'll leave you at the next village and then you won't get your apples."

That stopped her mare complaining, but it didn't stop the rain. While Cai chattered on about the great jousts they used to hold at Camelot before the Saxons came, Rhianna wrapped her cloak tightly around her and tried to recall the details of her dream. Look for the dragon… that could mean anything. There was a dragon on her shield. What did he mean by a spirit transfer? And what on earth was a pathfinder? She shook her head. As if she didn't have enough problems looking for Excalibur.

When she told Elphin about it, he frowned. "You probably dreamed of Merlin because we were talking about him earlier."

"But you said those stones had power," she reminded him. "What if it really was a message from Merlin? He might have come this way before us."

"Then he'll be at Camelot, won't he?" Elphin said. "And you can ask him yourself."

Cai shuddered. "I'm not surprised you had a nightmare about that dragon, Damsel Rhianna!" he said. "I did, too."

"See?" Elphin said, smiling at the squire. "That shadrake scared us all."

Rhianna sighed. Avalonians just didn't understand dreams.

Soon they turned on to a smooth stone track worn by wagon wheels, with many foot and hoof prints showing in the muddy parts. They crossed a bridge and passed a laden cart, whose driver cheered the knights on. Sir Bors pushed his horse into a canter, and Rhianna began to feel excited again. Her mother would be at Camelot, she remembered. Tonight they would sleep in dry beds and eat decent food. Cai's chatter was infectious, and even Sir Agravaine was smiling and joking with the others by the time they crested the final hill.

"Behold Royal Camelot, my lady!" Sir Bors said. But the words died on his lips, and he swore under his breath.

Rhianna's heart gave an uneasy thud.

The white walls were just as Cai had described, gleaming through the drizzle like a mist horse's coat, and damp banners flew from her towers. But her gates were firmly shut. They could see why. The ditches were dark with tents and makeshift shelters, while rough-looking men clad in soggy furs crawled up the lower terraces with siege catapults and ladders.

"Saxons!" Sir Agravaine growled. "Camped outside our very walls with their greedy eyes on Arthur's treasure, no doubt! How dare they?"

"The king's not here any more," Sir Bedivere said. "Who's to stop them?"

Sir Bors scowled at the dripping camp. "Well, they can sit there in the rain as long as they like! They won't get through Camelot's gates in a hurry!"

Sir Agravaine lowered his lance so it would

not be seen against the sky. He gave Rhianna a worried look. "With that lot down there," he said grimly, "neither will we."

◄❮❙ 5 ❙❯►

Bloodbeards

There one knight betrayed his lord,
Young Mordred of the bloodbeard horde,
In shadows of darkest Annwn bred,
Raised by a witch among the dead.

"**S**o what do we do now?" Sir Bedivere said
in dismay, turning his agitated horse in
circles, while Cai slid first one way and then the
other on its wet rump.

"We have to rejoin the other knights, that's
obvious," Sir Bors said. "Organise ourselves as

best we can and send that Saxon rabble packing. They're only half an army without Mordred's lot."

"Ride back to camp with her?" Sir Agravaine looked pointedly at Rhianna. "She'd be safer in a nunnery somewhere. Mordred's forces could be on their way back here even as we speak."

"Mordred was badly wounded in the battle. They'll tend to him first. And the Saxons are here, so there can't be many of them left hanging around the battlefield – it just might be the safest place of all right now."

"What if that witch-mother of his is still around, working her dark spells? We haven't got Excalibur any more. We don't even know if our camp's still there."

Sir Bors clenched a big fist. "Where else will the knights go, without Arthur? They ain't here at Camelot where they're needed, that's for sure!"

"Do you think the others will follow us?"

"They will when they see we've got Arthur's daughter."

"It's too dangerous…"

Rhianna got fed up with them arguing over her head as if she were some sort of trophy, instead of a girl with feelings who had only a few days ago seen the body of her murdered father. The sight of the barbarian army so close made her stomach churn and her blood rise. Her father had been fighting these men when he died, and now they were camped outside the walls of Camelot. If the knights didn't do something soon, her mother might be killed too.

She clenched her fists, making Alba prance. "Take me to the lake where you threw my father's sword, and when I've got Excalibur back

I'll lead you against the Saxons! I'm not afraid."

Cai gaped at her in admiration, and Elphin smiled.

But Sir Bors scowled. "Don't be so silly, girl! *You* lead the knights? Do you think King Arthur's sword is going to turn a half-grown damsel into a warrior, even if we can find it again, which I seriously doubt. The path to the lake vanished after the waters took it, and we ain't got time to go gallivanting about on foolish quests now. We had quite enough of that with the Grail… been a lot better off if we'd all stayed at home and kept our eyes on young Mordred, if you ask me."

"But Merlin said—"

"Merlin ain't here!" Bors growled. "And until he turns up, we can't risk no-one, Saxon or Briton, finding out who you are."

Just then, they heard the tramp of feet and rough voices coming up the hillside from the camp. Sir Bors cursed. "Enough chatter. We'd best get out of here fast, before them Saxons spot us! Cai, hold on tight – don't you dare fall off!"

Setting his heels to his horse, he led them away from the road at a pounding gallop into the fog. Sir Agravaine motioned them to follow, holding back his stallion to bring up the rear with the lance. Bedivere urged his chestnut after Sir Bors with a pale Cai clinging to his waist. Alba shook her damp mane and leaped after the bigger horses with an excited squeal. Elphin and Evenstar followed close behind. Rhianna forgot her frustration at the sight of the army and grinned as the mare's hooves stretched over the springy turf and the rain half-blinded her. This was nearly as much fun as their races back in Avalon!

When Sir Bors hauled his horse to a sudden stop, she almost galloped on past. But remembering what had happened to Merlin, she pulled up neatly behind him with the others. Then she saw what had stopped the knight: black wings gleaming through the rain ahead of them. At first, she thought the dragon had followed them. But she soon realised the wings were black metal at the top of a standard carried by a troop of wild-haired men on shaggy horses.

Sir Bors swore under his breath. "I *thought* we were being followed," he muttered. "That's Mordred's eagle – the young fool must think he's some sort of new-fangled emperor, sending his men riding about the countryside with it. Keep together!" he called, setting his heels to his horse again. "We'll lose them in this weather, if we're lucky."

Elphin flashed her a purple look, and they were off again.

As Alba passed Sir Bedivere's horse, Rhianna gave Cai an encouraging grin. The squire did not grin back. He was clinging to Sir Bedivere's cloak, bouncing like a sack on the poor chestnut's hindquarters. They heard a shout behind as Mordred's men gave chase, then Sir Bors led them downhill seeking cover. This was harder. As the hillside grew steeper and rockier, the mist horses balanced themselves with ease, Evenstar misting to avoid the rocks and Alba jumping them. But Sir Bedivere's horse stumbled and Cai lost his hold on the knight's cloak. He tumbled over the chestnut's tail and landed in a gorse bush with a yelp.

I am glad he was not riding me, Alba said.

Sir Bedivere's horse plunged on, the reins too slippery for him to stop. Sir Agravaine passed the boy at full gallop and yelled, "Stay down! They mightn't see you!" Sir Bors' bay had already vanished into the fog.

"Don't leave me!" Cai wailed.

Rhianna didn't hesitate. If these men had killed a king, they wouldn't stop at murdering a squire. She wheeled Alba, with Elphin and Evenstar close behind. Cai was running after them, screaming at them to stop, chased by a large black horse. As its rider raised his bow and took aim at the puffing squire, Rhianna headed Alba towards him and dragged the shield off her back. Behind her, Elphin pulled his harp out of its bag.

"Cai!" she called, throwing the shield at

the boy as she galloped past. "Catch!"

Cai dived for the shield, a look of relief in his eyes. But it turned out he could catch no better than he could ride. The shield slipped through his grasping hands and rolled under his pursuer's hooves, while the arrow – cheated of its target – hissed straight for Rhianna.

The first few notes from Elphin's harp glittered out into the rain, but too late. She just had time to hear Sir Bors yell a challenge as he galloped back up the gorge, and saw his sword flash out of its scabbard. Then the arrow thumped into her breast and she seemed to hang in midair while Alba raced on into the cloud.

Everything went very quiet. Surprisingly, there was no pain, just a warm glow that made her whole body tingle. She felt as if all she had to do was spread her arms and fly away.

Is this what it feels like to die? she thought.

Through a hole in the mist, she saw a ghostly figure standing on the crest of the hill staring at Camelot's towers. Light shimmered from his cloak and his flowing hair. He had his back to her but he seemed strangely familiar.

"Father…?" she whispered, afraid to break the spell.

The ghost turned his head and gave her a startled look.

Then sky and hillside whirled into one, and she started to fall.

◆◇◆

She came round lying on her back amidst a confusion of trampling hooves. Someone was sobbing. The sound reminded her of the Avalonians mourning King Arthur's death.

She brushed wet hair from her face and knocked the arrow off her breast. Remembering her vision, she quickly sat up and looked for the shining figure on the hill. But the ghost had gone.

"Girl's still alive!" someone grunted in surprise.

Hands gripped her elbows and dragged her up from her grassy bed, bringing her face to face with the winged standard. She swallowed her scream and shook her head to clear it of stars. Had she really seen her father's ghost? The strange warmth still tingled through her body. At least it had stopped raining.

Cai sobbed in the grip of a dark-haired man wearing a dented bronze breastplate. A second man had hold of Elphin. The Avalonian prince stood very erect and still, his purple eyes fixed on

Rhianna. Evenstar pawed the ground, held by a third man who had also taken Elphin's harp. Sir Bors' sword and the dragon shield were being examined by the leader of the group, who had blue spirals on his cheeks and a filthy, matted beard. Sir Bors knelt in the wet grass, his arms tied behind him and a fresh cut across his eye. A spear pricked his throat. Off in the mist she could hear the Saxons from the camp chasing the other two knights, and hoped they would get away.

"So... not dead after all," said the leader with an accent as wild as his looks. He tossed the shield to one of his men and fingered her Avalon armour where the arrow had bounced off. "Not only a damsel dressed up like a knight, but one who leads a charmed life, it seems." He leaned closer. His breath stank. "What's your name, lassie?"

Sir Bors stared at Rhianna with anguish in his eyes. "She's nobody, a girl we picked up from one of the villages is all—"

"No one asked you!" The leader clouted the big knight. "You've led us a merry dance through those cursed marshes. You'll get your chance to sing later. Right now, I'm talking to the maid." He bared his teeth at Rhianna. "I serve your new Pendragon, Prince Mordred. Men call us bloodbeards because we drink the blood of our enemies. If you don't want your companions' blood to fill our cups tonight, I suggest you answer."

Rhianna's heart twisted in fear for her friends, and she wanted to ask Elphin if he'd seen King Arthur's ghost too. But she stared the bloodbeard in the eye, her heart thumping. "Let them go, and then maybe I'll tell you."

He smiled coldly. "Oh, I think not. This is the Pendragon's shield. But where is Arthur's sword? Because Prince Mordred wants it. And what have you done with his body? Because Prince Mordred wants that, too. Well, the head at least... though maybe your champion's head would do instead?" He swung the sword at Sir Bors, and chuckled when the big knight flinched.

Rhianna glared at their captor. "Then Prince Mordred can't have what he wants!" she said. "Because the sword's at the bottom of a lake, and King Arthur's safe in Avalon."

She held her breath and eyed the hill again. Could her father's ghost hear her?

Elphin shook his head frantically at her. Sir Bors closed his eyes in despair. But Cai sniffed back his sobs and gave her a hopeful look – maybe he expected her to break free and overcome the entire troop of Mordred's bloodbeards and their Saxon friends single-handedly? She eyed the dagger their captors had confiscated from the squire, but soon gave up the idea. The fingers digging into her arms were too tight. For the first time in her life, she felt small. These men in their leather and bronze were so tall and strong. They towered over poor Elphin and Cai. Their scarred hands looked as if they could crush an Avalonian's bones.

The captain with his blue-painted face seemed even more frightening. He grinned again. "The maid's got more spirit than all Arthur's knights put together!" he said, giving her another blast of bad breath "Nice try, lassie, but I saw Prince Mordred kill the king with my own eyes. No doubt his knights have hidden his body someplace. No matter. We'll find it in the end, as we'll find his magic sword. A lake, you say? I don't suppose you happen to know which one?"

"No she don't," Bors said. "I told you, she's just some village girl we picked up on our way. Leave her alone!"

"But you do, maybe…" The bloodbeard gave him a sharp look. "No matter, you'll tell me later." He returned his attention to Rhianna. "Village girl, eh? Where did you get the fancy armour?"

She stole it, Elphin whispered under his breath, making the strings of his harp shiver.

"Steal it, did you?" said their captor, blinking as her friend's magic reached him.

Rhianna swallowed her angry words and glanced gratefully at Elphin. "Yes," she said.

"That's right! I, ah, stole it off a dead man on the battlefield. I…" What would a girl in the world of men want with armour? "I thought it looked pretty," she finished.

"Common thieves, then," the bloodbeard growled, losing interest in her. "Shame it looks too small for me. Does a good job, it seems – unlike your champion here." He kicked Sir Bors in the ribs, making the big knight grunt in pain.

Rhianna eyed the fallen arrow. Its head looked bent. Her Avalonian armour must have saved her life. At least its magic and Elphin's harp seemed to work in this world, even if they had lost Merlin. She breathed a bit easier. As long as their captors did not discover who she was, they might get a chance to escape.

The bloodbeard captain turned his attention

to Sir Bors. "Take them to the Saxon camp," he ordered. "Chief Cynric will want to question this knight once I've loosened his tongue. We might not have smoked Arthur's cowardly lot out of their hideout yet, but ten to one he knows where it is. We can trade the maid and the two boys for a couple of boats to dredge for the sword – Saxons are always after slaves. The plump one won't need much feeding." He poked Cai in the stomach with Sir Bors' sword and the squire moaned in fear.

As the men marched them at spear point towards the Saxon camp, their leader glanced at Elphin's horse, which had given up trying to mist for now. "See if you can find that other white pony. They don't look up to carrying much weight, but Cynric's men can always eat them if this siege drags on into the winter."

Rhianna glared at the bloodbeard captain. Eat Lord Avallach's mist horses? How dare he even suggest such a thing? "Run, Alba," she whispered. "Stay free."

◀◐ 6 ◑▶

Saxon Camp

Together the king and Mordred fell,
Excalibur blooded by a spell,
The saddest day in all the land
When the field went to the Saxon band.

Soon I'll wake up, Rhianna told herself, and all this will be nothing but a bad dream. Except she knew it wasn't a dream, and her legs trembled at the thought of meeting her father's enemies. Nobody in Avalon had ever fired an arrow at her, or jabbed her with a spear every time she opened her mouth to talk to her friends. If the world of men was like this, no wonder the queen had sent her to live with Lord Avallach.

Their captors separated Sir Bors and dragged him off with the two horses, making her afraid they might never see him again. She wondered what the bloodbeards would do to her friends if they found out who she really was. But as the smells and noise of the Saxon camp surrounded them, her fear turned to anger. These men had been responsible for her father's death. If they hadn't joined forces with Mordred, her cousin would never have got close enough to kill the king.

She looked hopefully back at the hill where she'd seen her father's ghost, but got another prod from a bloodbeard's spear. "Don't even think about rescue, lassie," he chuckled. "Your knights ran off. Cowards, the lot of 'em, now they've lost Arthur."

Rhianna saw Elphin's warning glance and bit off her angry words. Their only hope of getting out of here would be to get her friend's harp back. Until then she had to remember to act like a meek village girl so their captors would think her no threat. Easier said than done.

That evening Rhianna stood in the Saxon chief's tent fuming with helpless rage. The Saxons had taken her armour and replaced it with an old sack that hung raggedly around her knees. Her braid had come unravelled so that her hair frizzed to her waist. A leather slave-collar, which had been buckled around her neck, was rubbing her chin and making it sore.

Elphin and Cai wore similar collars, although they had at least been allowed to keep their own clothes. The Avalonian armour, her father's dragon shield, Cai's dagger, Sir Bors' sword and Elphin's harp made a glittering pile on a rug before the chieftain's feet. It seemed neither of her friends had seen King Arthur's ghost earlier, so she must have been dreaming after all. Either that, or it had fled when the Saxons swarmed over the hillside. The only good thing was that they hadn't caught Alba.

Chief Cynric turned out to be a huge man with yellow braids. His battle-scarred body was draped in furs. A heavy torque of gold finished by two huge rubies clasped his thick neck. He lounged in a chair with carvings of dragons on its arms, drinking from a horn and scowling at them. Rhianna decided the chair must have been stolen from one of her father's halls, because it looked too good for a barbarian tent.

"And what am I supposed to do with these young ragamuffins?" Cynric said to the bloodbeard captain, who had washed the blue spirals off his face but still stank. "I ask your people to find out where Arthur's men are hiding, and you bring me three half-grown children! I've got enough slaves."

"I thought you'd like to see them before I set them to work, my lord," said their captor in an oily tone. "The knight will be useful, won't he?"

"Only if he talks," Cynric pointed out. "Which he seems reluctant to do at the moment. And you say the others escaped? How many of them? The last thing we want is a troop of Arthur's knights charging in here looking for their friend."

"Two or three maybe," said the Saxon who had led the chase. "It was too foggy to see. They're just thieves and cowards, my lord, probably acting alone."

"Probably!" Cynric slammed his big hands down on the arms of his throne. "Maybe two or three? Too foggy to see? This whole campaign so far has been a string of probablies! Arthur's body was *probably* stolen away by that druid of his, but no one seems to know where. Several people have told me they saw Prince Mordred fall in the battle as well, yet no one seems to know where he is, either! Meanwhile, it seems these stubborn Britons are still not willing to open their gates and let me in. Do you want to know what I think? I think that snake Mordred has grown tired of his allies now we've helped him defeat Arthur, and is holed up someplace waiting for us all to go home so he can keep the fabled treasure of Camelot for himself."

"I don't think so, my lord," said their captor, frowning as the drunken Saxons laughed at him. He lifted Rhianna's frizzy braid. "Look, the maid's quite pretty under all that mud! She'll fetch a good price in the slave markets if you don't want her for yourself. And the dark boy is a bard with extra fingers, which some people value…" He eyed Cynric's scowl and added, "The knight will talk, I promise you. My men will make sure of it."

"If they don't kill him first," Cynric said with another glower. "I've heard about your methods, Bloodbeard." He put his head on one side and frowned at Rhianna. "I don't much care for the girl – she looks like she wants to kill me."

Rhianna could keep silent no longer. She lifted her chin. "I'll have a good try, Saxon thief, unless you take this collar off me and let my friends go!"

Cynric blinked at her in surprise, then threw back his head and laughed. "D'you hear that? Arthur and all his knights could not defeat me in battle, yet this freckle-faced maid dares call me a thief in my own camp! And what am I supposed to have stolen, girl?"

"Your tent is pitched outside King Arthur's home," Rhianna pointed out in a voice that carried easily over the laughter. "This is *his* land, not yours! But you're right about Camelot's treasure. Mordred wants Excalibur to give him power over men. Ask him – he's been sent to look for it!" She pointed at their bloodbeard captor.

Silence fell in the tent as the men all looked at their chief to see what he would do. Meanwhile, their captor swung his fist at her head. She ducked and he overbalanced, making the men laugh again. Catching his balance, he grabbed a handful of Rhianna's hair and forced her to her knees.

"Stupid girl's lying to save her skin. I'll soon teach her some manners, don't you worry, my lord," he growled.

Elphin began to hum under his breath.

But Cynric jumped to his feet. "Enough," he said, peering down at Rhianna with more interest. "Let the maid up and leave her with me. Save your energies for loosening that big knight's tongue. I want to know where Arthur's men are hiding before the sun rises, or you'll be the one kneeling before me with a slave collar around your neck. Understood?"

Her captor reluctantly let Rhianna go. She rubbed her head and glared at him as he hurried out of the tent. Cynric was still looking thoughtfully at her, and her stomach gave an uneasy flutter. Her and her big mouth… Why had she said that about Mordred wanting Excalibur for its magic? A village girl wouldn't have known that. They had to get out of this tent before the Saxon chief started asking awkward questions.

She glanced at Elphin, who nodded. Slowly, still humming under his breath, he walked across to the pile of their belongings and picked up his harp. Nobody stopped him. Cynric had leaned over the arm of his throne to talk in a low voice to one of his men. Rhianna felt for Cai's hand and gave it a squeeze. Tears of fear streaked the boy's face. "It'll be all right," she whispered. "We're going to get out of here, I promise. Block your ears when Elphin plays."

"Why's he going to play for them?" Cai whispered. "They're horrible."

But Cynric had finally noticed her friend. "Who said you could touch my things, boy?" he snapped, making his men look round.

Elphin met his glare calmly. "This harp sings only to my touch. No one else can play it like I can, my lord," he said in his soft voice. "Listen…" He stroked the strings with his slender fingers and sweet Avalonian music filled the tent.

Cynric's hands clenched on his throne. "I'll be the judge of that…" Then a look of wonder came over his face, and he waved back the men who had started towards the boy. "No, let him play. I'm in need of a new bard. Let's see what magic he's got in those extra fingers of his."

The men made space for Elphin on the end of a bench. He dared not look at them as he bent his head over his harp and concentrated on the magic. By the time he reached his third tune, Cynric's eyelids were drooping. Rhianna smiled as the sweet scent of enchantment briefly overcame the stench of the Saxon camp. Having heard the chief speak, Elphin had created the perfect lullaby for him. She nudged Cai, who – after staring in wonder at Elphin's swiftly dancing fingers – jammed his hands over his ears.

Chief Cynric opened his mouth in a huge yawn. Yawns are catching at the best of times. His men set down their drinking horns and yawned as well. Even Rhianna, used to the magic, had to fight to stay awake. She elbowed Cai again. The boy jumped.

"The trick is to hum different notes under your breath," she whispered. "And don't listen to the music. The spell isn't directed at us, but the dream magic can't be totally controlled." Cai's eyes closed again. "Never mind," she said. "I'll keep prodding you."

Elphin played on. When the last man had slumped over the benches, Rhianna unbuckled her collar and threw the hateful thing down on the rug. She and Cai ran to the pile of their belongings. Cai retrieved his dagger, their cloaks and the shield, while Rhianna dragged the Avalonian armour over her sack-dress and picked up Sir Bors' sword. She removed Elphin's collar for him while he kept playing and they hurried out of the tent.

The magic had worked on the sentries outside as well, but judging by the noise and firelit silhouettes further across the camp, it didn't reach very far. Rhianna hesitated at the flap. She looked back at the sleeping chieftain and his snoring warriors and smiled.

"Wait a moment," she whispered and tiptoed back to where Cynric snored on his stolen throne. She removed the Saxon chief's golden torque and slipped it round her own throat, then picked up the collar she'd worn and buckled it round the Saxon's thick neck. It only just fitted. She used the other two collars to strap his wrists to the arms of his throne, then ran back to join her friends.

"We're supposed to be thieves, aren't we?" she said. "If he thinks we've robbed him, maybe he won't realise who we really are."

Cai grinned. Elphin shook his head, but was concentrating too hard on his magic to say anything.

They made their way to the edge of the camp where the horses were tethered, letting the music take effect on any sentries before they ventured past. Progress was slow and Rhianna's impatience grew. She glanced over her shoulder at the chieftain's tent, afraid one of the men might wake up and raise the alarm. She wondered how they would ever find Sir Bors among this lot.

Then they saw the winged standard planted in the mud, and heard groans coming from a hut built against the wall of the ditch.

"They're killing him!" Cai yelled. Before they

could stop the squire, he had blundered inside. Rhianna cursed under her breath, gripped Sir Bors' sword and hurried after him, wishing it were not so heavy. Elphin followed, still playing his harp.

Smoke and shadows filled the hut. They glimpsed a sweaty Sir Bors, stripped to the waist and roped to a metal frame. The bloodbeard captain stood over him holding what looked like a black glove clamped around a glowing poker, while another man stoked a fire where more frightening tools lay heating. There was a horrible smell of burned flesh as the poker came down, drawing another desperate groan from Sir Bors. For a heartbeat, Rhianna thought she saw a second figure, standing behind the bloodbeard, dressed in glittering black armour.

"Let him go!" she ordered, unable to believe what the men were doing.

The bloodbeard captain spun round, saw the sword in her hand and swung his poker at it... or tried to. His arm jerked, the poker clanged to the floor and the black glove, which seemed to have a life of its own, flew across the hut and gripped her wrist. Its touch was ice cold. Rhianna shook the horrid thing off and ducked as a dark shape hissed past her out of the door. She heard a rushing noise like wind in the trees and thought she heard someone whisper, *"Excalibur"*. She looked round in sudden hope for her father's sword, but could see only shadows.

The bloodbeard yelled and dived after the glove. Now they could see it was a man's severed fist wearing a black gauntlet with a ring on its little finger. But before he could reach it, the captain fell under Elphin's spell and yawned. Rhianna put the sword to his throat and forced him backwards until he stumbled over his own poker and went down, dazed. The other bloodbeard seized a flaming stick from the fire and came at them, scowling. Then Elphin's music enchanted him, too, and with a shove from Cai he tripped over his friend and joined him in the land of dreams.

Cai used his dagger to free Sir Bors, who had slumped unconscious in his bonds. Rhianna stepped around the severed fist, feeling a bit sick. She wondered which poor prisoner it had belonged to. Her wrist had gone numb where the gauntlet had gripped it. With a grunt of effort, using both hands, she raised Sir Bors' sword over the man who had been torturing him.

"No, Rhia!" Elphin said, also eyeing the dark fist. "Blood will break the enchantment. Cai, go fetch the horses. I don't think I can keep this up much longer. We'll have to be quick."

As Cai ran outside again, Rhianna lowered the sword. The rushing noise faded, and she shook her head. What had she been thinking? King Arthur of the songs would never kill a sleeping man.

She cast the groaning bloodbeard a final glare. Then she took Sir Bors' shoulders, while Elphin took his feet. For once, Cai had been quick. Working together, they managed to heave the big knight across his horse's back. They used some of his cut bonds to tie him on. Then Elphin vaulted onto his mist horse, while Rhianna boosted Cai up on the bay behind the unconscious Bors. She put the reins in his hands.

"But I can't ride," Cai wailed.

"You'll have to," Rhianna told him. "Follow Elphin's horse."

"But what about you?"

"I'll ride my own horse." She slapped the bay on the rump. "Go!" she said, already running.

She had buckled Bors' scabbard around her waist, but even so the sword banged against her legs. The shield, though lighter, proved just as awkward to carry. She wondered how a knight managed in battle if they were unseated, and swore never to let that happen to her. She wished now she hadn't taken Cynric's torque because she didn't need the extra weight, and her wrist still felt numb. But she was angry with herself for causing them to get captured, as well as scared by what she had seen in the hut, so she kept up easily with the horses. Elphin played his harp as they went until they were past the last snoring sentry and trotting up the dark hillside into the fog.

"Alba!" she called softly. "Alba, you can stop misting now."

Just as her legs began to wobble from the effort of running and she started to think the mare had gone back to Avalon, the mist sparkled and Alba trotted out to meet them. Her reins were broken, but otherwise the little mare seemed unharmed. Evenstar gave a whinny of welcome. Rhianna dropped the sword and shield and threw her arms around her mist horse's neck. With her face buried in the damp mane, she trembled with relief. "I knew you wouldn't leave me, my beautiful one," she whispered.

Of course not, Alba said, indignant. *I want my apples.*

"Rhia," Elphin warned. "They'll be waking up soon. We have to go."

"Go where?" Cai said, clinging to the bay horse's mane with a worried look.

Rhianna strapped the dragon shield to Alba's saddle and mounted the mare. She searched the dark hillside in hope, but saw no sign of the other two knights. Merlin obviously wasn't at Camelot yet, either, or he'd have helped them. She looked longingly over her shoulder at the white towers that sheltered her mother. So close… but the queen should be safe enough, as long as nobody opened the gates before they got back.

She considered her friends' frightened faces, the fog and the unconscious knight. There was only one place she could think of to go now.

She took a deep breath and gave the squire a determined look. "We have to find the lake where Sir Bors threw away Excalibur," she said.

The Dark Fist

Mordred might have known something would go wrong.

His mother had shown him a trick with his missing hand, which his bloodbeards had rescued from the battlefield. With her help, using the spirit magic, he could send his shadow through the mists to rejoin it.

After a queasy time trying to leave his body, he found himself standing in a torchlit hut holding a red-hot poker over a groaning prisoner who was tied to a frame. He recognised the prisoner as one of Arthur's knights, Sir Bors, who used to bellow at him on the training ground and punish him for cheating in the jousts. He smiled as the poker hissed into the knight's shoulder.

Then, just as he was beginning to enjoy himself, three youngsters burst through the door. He glimpsed a tall, red-haired girl with a sword in her hand and forgot he wasn't really in the hut with her. He tried to seize her wrist and was flung back on his rocky bed.

"What happened?" he gasped, groping for the mirror. "Was that Excalibur?"

His mother frowned. "No, fortunately for us – but I think we might have underestimated Arthur's daughter."

"What do you mean? Just tell me what happened, woman! God, it *hurts*!" His missing fingers burned like tongues of fire. He wondered if that idiot bloodbeard had taken hold of the wrong end of the poker.

"Don't swear at me," his mother snapped. "I'm doing my best to help you. Now, you must try again."

"Why?" Mordred didn't see why he had to endure more pain just to spy on his own men. "Can't you send your shadrake again?"

"Forget the dragon!" snapped the witch. "The creature appears to have a mind of its own. If Merlin's tried the spirit transfer with a shadrake, he's crazier than I thought – but we don't need it any more. Use the power of your fist. Your man has no idea of the importance of the girl he captured. You must tell him before it is too late."

Mordred saw the sense in this. When the pain had eased, he sent his shadow back. It was easier this time. The captive knight had gone. Dawn showed at the door of the hut. The bloodbeards were sitting up, rubbing their eyes and yawning.

Mordred concentrated hard and made his gauntleted fist crawl across the floor to seize the captain's ankle. The man lifted a foot to kick the thing away, then froze as he saw Mordred's shadowy form in the doorway.

"M-master?" he whispered, rubbing his eyes again.

"Yes, it's me," Mordred snapped. "What are you up to? Where's the girl gone?"

"I… I'm not sure, Master. I had the strangest dream." The bloodbeard frowned at the empty frame and the cut ropes.

He groaned, as if only just noticing his prisoner had gone.

"That was no dream, you fool!" The effort of holding the man's ankle with his severed fist made Mordred even more impatient than usual. "She's escaped, hasn't she? Along with that knight you were questioning. Get after her! That 'village girl' you so stupidly left with the Saxon chief is King Arthur's daughter. I want her caught and brought to me at once. I hope you persuaded the knight to tell you what they did with my uncle's sword, because if my cousin gets hold of Excalibur before I do, your life won't be worth living. Go!"

Mordred tried to snatch up the poker to reinforce his message, but his control wavered. The hut vanished, leaving him panting and dizzy on his bed of rock.

"Good," his mother said from the mirror. "Unfortunately, I don't think you're strong enough yet to do that very often. But your men should be suitably motivated now.

Don't worry, my son. We have other tricks to play. Our troublesome damsel won't get much further."

◄0 7 0►

Battlefield

Ghosts and fears Rhianna did tame
To reach the lake with Nimue's name.
Her nerve was tested many times more
As she quested for that magic shore.

Though Rhianna wanted to gallop as fast and far from the Saxon camp as possible, she knew Cai would only fall off if they did. They trotted as fast as they dared, keeping the bay horse between them, while the boy cast nervous glances at the sky and muttered about

Mordred's spies flying in the dark. The night was very still and fog wrapped them in a damp blanket. To begin with, Rhianna couldn't think why it seemed so quiet. Then she realised Elphin had slipped his harp back into its bag, concentrating instead on making Evenstar mist across their prints to confuse their trail.

She started to worry about Sir Bors, who had not stirred since they'd rescued him from the Saxon camp. At first she hadn't really wanted the big knight to wake up, in case he stopped them going to the lake to look for the sword. But the further they went, the more unnatural his sleep seemed. What if they ran into another band of Mordred's men out here in the dark? Her wrist still felt cold where the dark gauntlet had gripped it. She didn't know if she could fight.

"Can't you heal him with your magic?" she whispered to her friend, glancing at the unconscious knight.

Elphin shook his head. "Sorry, Rhia." His reins lay loose on his horse's neck, and she noticed spots of blood in Evenstar's mane.

"Your hands!" she said in concern.

He curled his blistered fingers in embarrassment. "It's the strings," he explained. "I couldn't stop playing, or we wouldn't have got out of the Saxon camp. It never used to happen in Avalon."

"You should have said something." She felt angry again. Why hadn't Merlin warned them magic had a price in the world of men? Then she remembered Lord Avallach giving final instructions to her friend before they left Avalon, when she had been so impatient to get going.

Elphin must have known the consequences of using magic all along, but he had still played his harp so they could escape.

He gave her a weary smile. "And let those Saxons find out who you were and use you as a hostage? My father would never forgive me." He added in a low tone, "Besides, I can't just keep playing my harp out here. If anything is following us, the music will give us away for sure. It's not only dragons we need to worry about. There was darker magic than mine at work in that hut… Don't say anything to him, but Cai might be right about Mordred's spies."

Rhianna thought of the shadowy figure she'd seen in the hut and shivered. She pulled her cloak tighter. As they rode, her wrist that the gauntlet had touched grew colder. She slipped it under her Avalonian armour, which seemed to help a bit. She didn't make a fuss. If Elphin realised, he'd only insist on playing his harp to heal her, and his fingers were in a worse state than her wrist was. She hoped Excalibur might work some magic on it once they got to the lake.

She eyed Cai, who had been unusually quiet since they left the camp. "You do know where you're going, don't you?" she asked. The last thing they needed was to get lost out here in the dark and ride into another band of Mordred's bloodbeards.

The squire chewed his lip. "Sort of. I know the way to the battlefield, anyhow. The lake should be close to there."

"Then what's wrong?"

"It was my fault we got captured," he said in a small voice. "I should have stayed hidden in the bushes like Sir Agravaine told me to, only I was so scared I couldn't think right." He sniffed. "I'm glad you came back for me, Damsel Rhianna. I'll never be a brave knight like my father was."

Rhianna sighed. "No, it was my fault – I should have waited for the knights before coming back to help you. I never thought those bloodbeards would actually shoot me." Another shiver went through her. If it hadn't been for her magic armour, Elphin would even now be on his way back to Avalon with her body, and Mordred would have all the time in the world to find Excalibur. "Besides, you're doing just fine," she added, shaking the thought away. "You're riding now, aren't you?"

Cai looked down at his horse in surprise. Coming over the hills, he had clung to the ropes securing the unconscious knight and let the bay horse follow the two mist horses. But once they had left the hills behind and descended out of the fog into a wooded valley, he had taken up the reins and was now trotting out in front.

"I am!" He grinned in delight. "Just wait till the other squires see me! Shall we go a bit faster?"

He gave the bay a kick in the ribs, and the big horse leaped forward as it had obviously been trained to do in a joust. Cai lost his balance and tumbled off over its tail.

That stallion is stupid, Alba observed, as the bay horse trotted off with Sir Bors. *I would not leap like that with an inexperienced rider.*

"No, you misted with me instead," Rhianna reminded the mare. But she had to smile as the squire jumped up and ran after the horse.

It reminded her of how she'd learned to ride Alba, falling off until she got fed up with the bruises and finally managed to stay on.

"I think you'd better learn to gallop another day, Cai." Elphin winked at Rhianna as he dismounted to boost the boy back into the saddle again. "For now, just concentrate on not getting us lost."

"You concentrate on keeping that dragon off me, fairy boy!" Cai scowled at the Avalonian. "That's obviously why my horse is so jumpy today."

Rhianna fought a smile.

They rode in silence for a while, each lost in their own thoughts. Several times Rhianna thought she heard large wings beating overhead in the dark, but she kept quiet. Cai was spooked enough already. She thought instead of the shining figure she'd seen outside Camelot's walls when the arrow had hit her. Had it really been her father's ghost, or just her imagination?

At dawn, they crested a hill and saw the battlefield below them. A river wound across the plain under a layer of drifting crimson mist. Ravens circled and cawed overhead. As the sun cleared the ridge, she realised the lumps she'd assumed to be dozing sheep were dead men, their bones pale in the early light.

"Which way's the lake?" she asked, feeling a bit sick.

"Dunno." Cai frowned. "But it can't be very far. Sir Bedivere ran there and back again at least three times before Sir Bors took Excalibur off him to throw it in."

Rhianna gritted her teeth and headed Alba down the slope.

She tried not to look at the bodies they passed, but the ravens' cries made her neck prickle, and the smell was *awful*. She covered her mouth as she rode. Dead men lay where they had fallen, with lances and arrows sticking out of them and empty sockets where the birds had pecked out their eyes. The mist horses snorted and danced sideways, unused to such things.

I do not like it here, Alba said, picking up her delicate feet as high as she could.

Fortunately for Cai the bay horse had been battle trained and trotted steadily past the bodies, but the boy clung to its mane as if afraid the dead men would rise up to grab his ankles. Elphin's fingers tightened on his reins, his eyes deep purple.

Rhianna began to see why Lord Avallach disapproved of fighting. What if Merlin didn't turn up, and she had to lead her father's knights against Mordred's army, after all? She wondered if she would ever have the stomach to take part in a battle like this one, even if she managed to find Excalibur and persuaded someone to teach her how to use it.

Then she remembered Mordred's man torturing Sir Bors in the hut, and set her jaw. If she met the bloodbeard on a battlefield with a magic sword in her hand, maybe she would feel differently.

About halfway to the river, they entered a patch of mist. She felt a strange tingling in her spine, and her Avalonian armour grew warm. She reined Alba to a halt.

Elphin stopped Evenstar at her side. "What's wrong?"

"I don't know. Feels like magic—"

Even as she spoke, the air shimmered. She closed her eyes, suddenly dizzy, and found herself in one of Merlin's song-pictures.

Ghostly warriors fought all around her. Men's swords flashed down and their mouths moved, but there was no sound as they died. Then a big horse came galloping out of the sun, ridden by a knight in black armour wielding an axe. His eyes glittered green through a slit in his helm, from which a black plume trailed like wings.

For a heartbeat she sat Alba in the path of the horse, frozen with terror. Then she dragged Bors' sword out of its scabbard and swung it clumsily at the dark knight. The heavy blade passed straight through him and slipped out of her hand to land, shivering, in the grass. She reached down to retrieve it, and her breath stopped in her throat. Almost under Alba's hooves lay the man she'd last seen in the bottom of Merlin's boat. His head was bare and blood ran down his face. His hands clasped a shining sword...

"Father!" she cried, swinging her leg over the saddle to help him.

"Rhia!" Elphin's hand caught her elbow, jerking her back. "Ignore them! They can't hurt you. They're just confused souls who don't want to leave their bodies because they died before their time in the battle. The Wild Hunt will take them into the mists when it rides into the world of men at midwinter. It must be your armour making them visible – look, it's shining. Pull your cloak over it. I think we should get off this battlefield."

"Me too," Cai said.

"No, wait!" Rhianna spun Alba round on the spot, looking in vain for the wounded king.

"This is where my father died."

Elphin gave her a sharp look. "Are you sure?"

"How do you know?" Cai said.

"I know, all right? And they took Excalibur that way... across the river." Her heart quickened as she glimpsed a pale figure on the far bank beckoning to her. But before she could see if it was her father, a dark cloud passed over the water and the ghost vanished on an icy wind.

Drawn by their voices, hoof beats thundered towards them. Elphin's hand flew to his harp as two knights cantered out of the mist. Still dizzy from her vision, Rhianna reached desperately for the dropped sword. Then the bay horse whinnied to the newcomers and she relaxed.

"Sir Agravaine!" Cai said in relief. "Sir Bedivere!"

Sir Agravaine gave the three of them an equally relieved look. "We've been following you for ages. You're more difficult to track than a herd of unicorns!" He frowned at the unconscious Sir Bors. "What did those devils do to him back there? No, don't tell me. I can guess. You can tell us how you escaped later. Right now we'd best get off this battlefield before anyone spots us. There's Saxon boats coming upriver." He set his heels to his stallion and pounded away across the plain.

Still disturbed by her vision, Rhianna held Alba back, staring anxiously at the river. But her father's ghost had gone, and her friends were already galloping after Sir Agravaine. Before she could gather her thoughts, Alba gave a little squeal and leaped after the others.

By some miracle, Cai was still on the

bay horse's back when they pulled up in a woodland glade. Thousands of flies, bred on the battlefield, buzzed in the air. Golden leaves steamed sweetly in the autumn sunshine. Their horses snorted in relief to be away from the smell of the dead.

"All right now?" Elphin whispered.

Rhianna nodded. "I dropped Sir Bors' sword," she admitted.

"Don't worry about it," Sir Bedivere said. "We'll get it back when the Saxons have gone. Poor old Bors isn't in any fit state to use it yet, anyway. Did those bodies give Damsel Rhianna a funny turn?"

Rhianna opened her mouth to tell them about King Arthur's ghost, then changed her mind. She didn't feel ready to think about all those men who had died fighting in her father's last battle, let alone the dark knight. "Yes," she said rubbing her wrist, which had gone cold again. "It's the first time I've been on a battlefield."

Cai gave her a sympathetic look. "You did better than me. I was sick my first time."

Sir Agravaine dismounted to examine Sir Bors, who had begun to groan, though he still showed no sign of waking. "Looks like we could all do with some rest. We should be safe enough from Mordred's spies under the trees. We'll stop here for a bit, let them boats pass before we ride on up to our camp – we don't want anyone following us there. Ought to find out what those Saxons are up to, as well."

"They're probably looking for Excalibur," Rhianna said, making an effort to pull herself together. "Mordred's men said something about dredging the lake for it. It's across the river, isn't it? We should go there now, before they find it."

"I agree," Elphin said. "The bloodbeards tortured Sir Bors back in the camp. He might have told them where to look."

"Absolutely not," Sir Agravaine said. "Bors would never talk, and the bloodbeards won't find the path without one of the Pendragon blood. Damsel Rhianna's in no state to go swimming after a magic sword. We've only just got you back from the Saxons. We're not about to risk losing you a second time."

"Look, there's still some blackberries left!" Sir Bedivere said, seeing their disappointed faces. "We'll make camp here until Sir Bors wakes up and let him decide, how about that?"

Rhianna eyed the unconscious knight and

frowned. He didn't look as if he'd wake up any time soon. Cai had already dismounted and was gathering the juicy blackberries, stuffing them into his mouth as fast as he picked them. She watched him for a moment, wondering how he could possibly eat so much after what they'd just ridden past. Then the trees tipped sideways, and she found herself lying in a bed of leaves with Alba's nose breathing anxiously in her ear.

I am sorry, I misted. I am trying to remember not to.

Elphin knelt beside her and put his hand on her forehead. It reminded her of when the branch had knocked her off back in Avalon. She pushed it away. "Don't fuss," she said. "I'll be all right, but we have to get to that lake before Mordred's men. I think I know the way now…" She told him how she'd seen

King Arthur's ghost beckon to her.

Elphin listened gravely. For a moment she didn't think he believed her. Then he nodded. He glanced at the knights, who were lowering Sir Bors to the ground. "Best wait until dark to make sure no one follows us. Leave it to me."

꧁꧂

Later, Sir Agravaine took Cai back to the battlefield to collect Sir Bors' sword. They returned with a pile of spare weapons and reported that the Saxon boats had stopped for the night. Sir Bors looked a bit better, sleeping more naturally now. Rhianna joined her friends around the fire as they shared out the last of the blackberries. She tucked her cold legs under her.

"Tell me about my father's sword," she said.

"Why did he ask you to throw it away?"

"God knows," Sir Agravaine growled. "Though Merlin probably put him up to it… druid stuff, no doubt. Mind you, if young Bedivere had his way, we'd still have Excalibur and Soft Hands here to lead us!"

Sir Bedivere flushed. "I didn't want to keep it for myself."

"Just as well, because you'll never be strong enough to control it."

Sir Bedivere smiled, acknowledging this. "Have you heard the story of how your father drew Excalibur from a stone to become king, Damsel Rhianna?"

Rhianna nodded. "Everyone knows that old story."

They had a song in Avalon that told of how, as a boy, Arthur had amazed everyone by freeing the sword from a rock when no grown knight could shift it. It would be an easy enough trick for an Avalonian, of course, and no doubt Merlin had used his magic to help her father back then.

"But I still don't understand how Excalibur gives the Pendragon power over men," she said. "How does the magic work, exactly? Cai told us it feeds on souls…"

"It does!" Cai said. "Except for King Arthur, anyone who touches Excalibur dies a horrible death."

"That's not quite true, Cai," Sir Bedivere said. "Plenty of men tried to pull it out of the stone before Arthur did. King Arthur gave it to me when he was dying, and Sir Bors took it up to the lake. We're not dead, are we?"

They looked uneasily at the sleeping knight.

"That's not because he touched Excalibur," Sir Bedivere said quickly. "I wrapped it up in my cloak to be on the safe side."

"It fed on those Saxons' souls all right," Sir Agravaine said with a chuckle. "Excalibur's supposed to give the Pendragon the strength of a hundred men, and I saw Arthur kill at least a hundred of the barbarians before he died, so the sword works fine. Just as well it's lying at the bottom of an enchanted lake, if you ask me. God help us all if Mordred ever gets hold of it."

Rhianna sighed. Obviously the knights didn't know how the magic worked any more than she did.

"If Excalibur gave my father the strength of a hundred men, then how come Mordred managed to kill him?" she asked, thinking uneasily of her vision on the battlefield.

"Everyone knows his witch-mother worked a dark spell on the sword," Cai said. "King Arthur was really aiming for the little sneak's neck, but Excalibur turned aside at the last moment and just chopped off Prince Mordred's hand instead."

"That's squires' gossip, Cai," Sir Bedivere said, frowning at the boy. "I'm sure Damsel Rhianna doesn't want to hear all the gory details. Now then, you youngsters had best get some sleep. It's a long ride up to camp and we'll be making an early start."

Rhianna opened her mouth to say she did want to hear all the details, especially any that had to do with dark spells on the sword, since she'd soon be holding it herself. But Elphin reached for his harp and winked at her. "I'll play something to help Sir Bors sleep," he offered, setting his blistered fingers to the strings.

As the sweet Avalonian music tinkled into the night, Rhianna curled up in her cloak and closed her eyes. She felt bad about making her friend play again so soon with his sore hands. But if the knights wouldn't help them find the lake, they had no choice but to find it themselves.

She meant to stay awake until Elphin's music had enchanted everyone. But the strain of their escape caught up with her, and she drifted into a muddled dream where her father's ghost and Sir Bors were arguing in the trees near the camp. They kept looking at her, but she couldn't hear their words. And when she tried to raise her head to see them better, the dark fist she'd seen in the Saxon camp grabbed her hair and dragged it back down.

She woke with a start in the middle of the night. A hand covered her mouth. She tasted blood, and her heart pounded with panic. She stiffened, determined not to be taken as a Saxon slave again.

"Hush, Rhia, it's me." Elphin whispered in her ear. He took his hand away and helped her sit up. "We'd better hurry if we're going to find your lake before the knights wake up."

Her heart steadied when she saw their mist horses waiting saddled in the moonlight. She must have been more tired than she'd thought to let Elphin's music enchant her, too. She tiptoed after her friend, eyeing the sleepers. Cai's blackberry-stained cheeks glowed in the firelight. The three knights moaned and shifted in their sleep.

"They'll wake if anyone attacks, don't worry,"

Elphin whispered as they mounted. "I didn't work a very strong spell on them – my fingers are too sore. Though it seemed to work on you all right, sleepyhead! Any dreams?"

"I dreamed I saw my father talking to Sir Bors," she told him.

Elphin nodded. "It's possible, if we're getting close to one of the Lights. Keep your eyes open."

They rode in silence. Rhianna hoped for another glimpse of King Arthur's ghost, but only the moon shone through the trees to guide them. The moonlit forest and rustling night creatures reminded her of Avalon, and she almost forgot they were in the land of men being hunted by a dragon and Mordred's bloodbeards. Then she saw the place on the riverbank where the ghost had beckoned to her.

Excitement tingled through her.

"This is it!" Without waiting for her friend, she headed Alba down the bank. The mare sniffed at the running water suspiciously. But her hooves glittered with enchantments as she stepped delicately on to the surface and trotted out into the middle. Rhianna smiled, relieved the Avalonian magic still worked in the land of men. Then she heard a splash and a surprised snort behind her. She looked round in concern.

Elphin held Evenstar on a tight rein. The horse's legs were dissolving into mist. "I can't go any further with you, Rhia," he said quietly. "The Saxons stole my horse's shoes back in the camp. I didn't tell you before because you'd probably have made us go back for them, knowing you."

She stared at her friend in dismay. Mist horses could swim no better than their Avalonian riders. "You can't ride Evenstar back to Avalon without them!"

"I know. But if all goes well tonight, at least you'll have Excalibur. I can't see your ghost, anyway. I'll wait here for you and keep an eye on those Saxons. My harp still sings with blood on the strings. If you hear it, stay hidden until the knights wake up." He managed a brave smile.

Rhianna wanted to kiss him. Instead, she untied the dragon shield from her saddle and made him take it. She gave him the Avalonian gesture of respect. "I never thanked you for getting us out of that Saxon camp. I thought your harp would be useless against armed men, but now I see why Lord Avallach sent you with me. *Faha'ruh*, Elphin."

He took the shield with another smile. "Save your thanks for after you've found your father's sword. You're going to have to swim. Rather you than me."

"I like swimming," she reminded him. She eyed her friend's blisters doubtfully. "I'll be as quick as I can. Will you be all right?"

"I'm a prince of Avalon," Elphin said with a grin. "Don't worry about me. Worry about yourself, Rhianna Pendragon. You're mortal remember?"

Alba trotted quietly across the moonlit river, watched by a startled swan. Rhianna felt very exposed as she cantered the mare up the slope on the other side. But Elphin's music tinkled after her, wrapping them in enchantments, and she reached the trees safely.

She hesitated, wary of the narrow paths

where enemies could be waiting to ambush them. Then she saw a shining figure between the trunks and smiled. "Father?" she whispered. But the ghost merely beckoned and glimmered deeper into the wood. She put the stolen horseshoes out of her mind and urged Alba into a trot, determined not to lose him.

Her ghostly guide led her along a twisting path, always too far ahead to see his face. Soon she saw a gleam of silver water through the trunks, and they emerged into moonlight again, where the ghost vanished. Rhianna caught her breath in wonder. Despite her worry that Mordred's men might have found the lake first, there was no sign of boats up here. Rainbows danced over the surface, reminding her of Lord Avallach's palace. In the magical warmth, white lilies bloomed around the shore.

She dismounted, stripped off her armour and laid it over Alba's saddle. She put the golden torque she'd stolen from the Saxon chief on top and bundled her cloak around them. She rubbed her numb wrist and scowled at her sack-dress. Somehow, she'd imagined looking a bit more regal when she recovered Excalibur. Never mind. Nobody would see her.

"Don't let anyone catch you," she warned the mare, looping the reins over the saddle.

Of course not! I will graze this sweet grass while I wait.

She gave Alba a kiss to let the mare know she forgave her for not telling her about Evenstar's lost shoes. Then she took a deep breath and dived into the moonlit water.

◅ 8 ▻

Lady of
the Lake

Riddles four must she answer right
To claim the famous Sword of Light.
Only the blade bloodless and clean
May once again in Avalon gleam.

The lake was warmer than she'd expected.
Rhianna swam as quietly as she could,
using a circular stroke she'd taught herself back
in Avalon to avoid splashing. Water slipped

over her skin like liquid silver. The sack-dress swirled around her legs, but was short enough not to tangle them. Moonlight danced in the ripples she made. She kicked strongly, delighting in the stretch of her body and the rhythm of her stroke. She'd missed this. Just her and the water, alone with her thoughts.

As she began to wonder how she'd ever find the sword, she saw a glimmer in the depths like an underwater star. Just as well the Saxons had not reached the lake first. A shiver went through her as she remembered their big hands on her, and how close she had come to failing her quest before she'd even started. Treading water, she peered between her feet to check she had the right place. Then she took a huge gulp of air and dived towards the glimmer.

It was a long way down, much further than

she'd thought. Her lungs ached to breathe. But the light grew brighter all the way, until she recognised the white jewel and shining blade from Merlin's song-pictures. Excalibur! The sword had fallen part way under a rocky shelf. She groped under the rock and reached for the hilt. But as she touched it, a pale hand appeared out of the shadows and snatched it from her grasp.

She watched in disbelief as the hand pulled the sword under the shelf. Had Mordred's witch-mother worked some dark magic and lured her down here to drown? Her heart gave an uneasy thud. But the hand was too small to be human, and the fingers had little webs between them.

No you don't! She needed to take another breath. But if she went back to the surface now, she'd lose sight of the sword. She gritted her teeth. Pulling herself under the rock, she swam into the tunnel after her disappearing prize.

She could see nothing beyond the hand that had taken it. Something cold and scaly brushed her cheek. Rhianna shuddered, but forced herself to keep swimming. Her lungs began to hurt. Little flashes of light stabbed her eyes. What if she got stuck in the tunnel and drowned down here? Suddenly, leaving the knights in an enchanted sleep didn't seem such a good idea. But they probably couldn't swim anyway, not with all the armour they wore under their cloaks.

She resisted a crazy urge to giggle and realised she could see again. The tunnel had ended in a large underwater cavern where blue and green glitters danced in the water. She swam upwards with the last of her strength, and her head broke the surface. She gulped lungfuls of air. Treading water, she wiped wet hair from her eyes and blinked around in amazement.

At first she thought she'd found a way back to Lord Avallach's palace. The colours flashed and danced in the same way. But instead of a crystal dome, rock arched overhead glittering with coloured jewels. The light came from glowing sea anemones that waved feathery tendrils from the cavern walls. A little beach sloped up to a cave with strings of shells hung at the entrance. The thief who had taken her father's sword sat on a rock at the water's edge staring at Rhianna with interest.

Rhianna couldn't help staring back. She knew it wasn't polite, but she had never seen a lady with a fish's tail before, not even in Avalon. Except for the webs between her fingers, the fish-lady seemed human enough from the waist up. She had shimmering green hair that wrapped her pale body like a cloak. From the waist down, she had a beautiful tail crusted with jewels like the rock. She wore a necklace of pink shells, and more shells dangled from her ears. Excalibur rested across her lap, the white jewel on its hilt shining more brightly than ever.

Rhianna swam cautiously to the beach, wondering if she could snatch the sword and dive back through the tunnel before the fish-lady caught her. But the webbed fingers curled possessively around the hilt, as if she had guessed Rhianna's thoughts.

The turquoise eyes sparkled with amusement as she spoke. "I didn't expect a girl. You must have unusually good lungs to make it through the tunnel."

"You made it through," Rhianna pointed out, having finally caught her breath. "What are you doing with that sword? It belongs to King Arthur."

"Not any more," said the fish-lady. "It was offered to me after his death, as all warriors offer their most powerful weapons to the spirits of the water. I am the lady of this lake, whom men call Nimue. And you are…?"

"King Arthur's daughter," Rhianna said, finally remembering her manners. "Rhianna Pendragon. But my father's not dead yet. The knight who threw the sword away made a mistake. I've come to fetch it back for him."

"Rhianna Pendragon," the fish-lady repeated, and the name sang around the cavern, making the anemones flare brightly. "Hmm. A damsel with a warrior's name. You have the smell of

Avalon on you, it's true, but no extra fingers. No tail either, I see," she observed, as Rhianna squeezed the water from her hair.

"Of course I haven't got a tail!" Rhianna said. "I'm human. And I need that sword so we can take it back to Avalon for my father as soon as Merlin shows up again."

"Ah…" The lady's turquoise eyes went distant. "Dear old Merlin. Strange, I can't see him. How is he?"

"He got lost in the mists coming over from Avalon. That's why he's not here with me now. Something went wrong. There was a dragon and I think it's following us, but my father's ghost showed me the way…" She frowned, still not quite sure of what she'd seen. "I haven't time to talk, I'm afraid. We're supposed to be meeting Merlin at Camelot. Please can I have the sword,

Lady Nimue? I've got Pendragon blood so it won't harm me."

She bit her lip. *Hopefully not, anyway.*

Nimue laughed, a tinkling laugh that made the anemones flare again. "You might find it harder than you think to take the Sword of Light back to Avalon. Its magic has been tainted by its use here in the world of men. Merlin ought to realise that. I wonder what he's up to bringing you here to look for it, an untrained damsel… A dragon, did you say?"

Rhianna flushed. "I'll fight the dragon if I have to!" she said. "I'm not afraid."

The fish-lady sobered. "I didn't think you were, Rhianna Pendragon," she said. "I can tell you're not the sort of girl to scare easily. Not many humans would have swum through that tunnel after me without a single breath of air in their body. You can't even breathe underwater like me, can you?" She lifted her green hair, and with a start Rhianna saw three little flaps of skin flutter on her neck… gills, like a fish.

She shook her head, feeling a bit queasy.

"No, you're human enough," Nimue continued. "I believe you might even have Pendragon blood, as you claim. And you're certainly brave enough. But do you really mean to take Excalibur back to your father in Avalon, or are you just trying to get hold of the sword for your own purposes? This blade was forged by non-human hands. The hilt is strong in spirit magic. Do you think you can control it? Or will it turn on you as it turns on its enemies?" She stroked the glimmering jewel with her webbed fingers.

"I don't tell lies!" Rhianna said. "And I grew up in Avalon, so I think I can handle a magic blade."

"Oh you do, do you?" Nimue gave her an amused look. "Even your father had a struggle with it at first. Merlin had to sheathe its blade in stone before young Arthur could lay his hands safely on the hilt. Hmm. You're human and will die if you lose your soul, so I think I'd better give you a test to make sure."

She rested the sword's glittering tip against the rock. Rhianna stiffened. Did Nimue mean her to pull it out of the stone, like her father had done? Elphin might be able to sing it out for her, but he'd never make it through that underwater tunnel. She felt dizzy after holding her breath for so long, and her wrist was still cold where Mordred's gauntlet had gripped it. But she flexed her shoulders. She'd just have to grab Excalibur and swim as fast as she could. She'd be all right once she was back in Alba's saddle.

Nimue smiled again. "Don't look so worried, Rhianna Pendragon. You've already proved your strength by following me through the tunnel. Your test will be of the spirit. If you can answer four riddles, then you can take your father's sword back with you into the world of men. Ready?"

Rhianna eyed the blade. It seemed she had no choice. She raised her chin and met the fish-lady's gaze. She nodded.

"What is the name of the Sword of Light?" asked Nimue.

Rhianna smiled. Easy one. "Excalibur!" she said.

The anemones flared blue in approval, and

Nimue immediately asked her second riddle: "Who carries the Lance of Truth?"

Rhianna hesitated. She remembered Merlin speaking of the four Lights back in Lord Avallach's hall. But she had been seeing Mordred's axe coming down on her father's head at the time and not really paying attention. *The Lance of Truth made by the hands of men.* Merlin had told them it was broken, but she was pretty sure the druid hadn't mentioned who carried it.

"Er... a knight?" she guessed, hoping the fish-lady wouldn't want someone's name. The anemones flared again, less brightly.

Nimue's eyes narrowed. "Good enough for now, I suppose. I have a feeling the Lance will change hands soon, anyway, now it's been broken. What is the secret of the Crown of Dreams?"

"The jewel of Annwn," Rhianna said, more confident now. Another flare of light rippled around the underwater cavern.

"And what does the Grail contain?"

Rhianna closed her eyes, dizzy again. There had been another question: Who commands the Grail? But that wasn't what Nimue wanted to know. She tried to remember the exact words of Merlin's song. "Stars...?" she ventured, then shook her head. No, that wasn't right. 'Said' to hold all the stars in Heaven. There had been no picture of the Grail in Lord Avallach's walls. No one knew, not even Merlin.

"I don't know," she said in the end, bowing her head. She had failed. Now she would have to snatch the sword and hope the fish-lady didn't catch her in the tunnel.

Nimue gave a long sigh. She regarded

Rhianna thoughtfully over the shimmering blade. "You pass the test."

Rhianna glanced up, surprised.

"You've the same mixture of innocence and bravery Arthur had as a boy." Nimue smiled. "The Grail reveals itself in its own time. The Sword of Light will give you quite enough to think about for now. Do you know why it was returned to me here, and not taken to Avalon with King Arthur's body?"

Rhianna frowned at her use of the word 'body'. "Sir Bors said he threw it into your lake because it was my father's dying wish."

"Exactly. Arthur told his knights to return it to me because the blade had been blooded. He knew it could not return to Avalon while Mordred's blood stained it."

Rhianna froze. "Then I can't take the sword

back for my father, after all… Merlin lied to me!"

Nimue shook her hair, and turquoise drops showered around them. "Merlin is a druid. He does not lie. He just twists the truth sometimes to suit his purposes. I'm not sure why he brought you here to collect Excalibur when I'd have given it to him, had he asked me nicely enough. But no doubt he has his reasons. I can't do much about the hilt I'm afraid, but I have cleansed the blade. Though if you want to take it back to Avalon to help your father, you must not allow a single drop of blood to dim its light." She smiled at Rhianna's expression. "Ah, I see Merlin forgot to tell you that, too? Perhaps he thought you'd never use the sword in anger, anyway, seeing as you're a girl."

"But—" Rhianna began, and bit her lip.

She had been going to ask what use a sword would be that could not be blooded. But, of course, it could be blooded. King Arthur had used it against his enemies. Not if she wanted to take it back to Avalon, though, where blood broke enchantments. That made sense, she supposed. She thought of her dream at the stone circle. *Do not try to use the sword.* Was that what Merlin had meant – do not blood it?

Very faintly, they heard music in the rippling air. The fish-lady gazed intently at the cavern wall. She held out Excalibur, hilt first. "You must go quickly now. Your friend needs you."

Rhianna eyed the white jewel, remembering Nimue's warning about the spirit magic, and what Cai had said about Excalibur feeding on souls. Well, if it did eat her soul then at least she wouldn't end up in Annwn. She took a quick breath and grasped Excalibur firmly with her left hand. The hilt fitted comfortably in her palm and the anemones gave a rustling sigh, as if an invisible audience approved. As Nimue let go, the blade glimmered and warmth flowed up her arm. The numbness in her wrist vanished.

She lifted the sword curiously and tried a couple of cuts through the rippling air. It was light in her grip, completely different from Sir Bors' clumsy blade. She could manage it easily with one hand. It made her feel like dancing. She laughed and twirled up the beach, slicing at invisible enemies and trailing ribbons of silver light.

"Rhianna Pendragon!" snapped Nimue. "Have you forgotten your friends already?"

The light around her died, and she came back to herself with a start. She thought of

Elphin waiting on the riverbank, alone and unarmed, keeping watch on the Saxon boats.

A little out of breath, she smiled. "Thank you for the sword, Lady Nimue. I won't forget about the blood. I don't want to fight anyone with it, anyway. I just want it to give my father the strength to fight Mordred when he is reborn."

Nimue sighed again. "I wish you luck, child. But take care. Mordred will not like you beating him to the Sword. Remind Merlin to make you a scabbard for it when you next see him. You can't carry Excalibur around in the world of men spilling its magic everywhere. Now, go! The sword will light your way out."

It was easier going out than in. Rhianna had more air in her lungs and the Sword of Light to guide her. She swam carefully, so she would not chip the blade on the rocky walls of the tunnel, thinking of Nimue's warning. But she couldn't help a grin of triumph. She'd finally done something an Avalonian couldn't do, not with all their magic. It felt good.

The sky above the lake seemed very bright after the tunnel. When her head broke the surface, she had to squint until her eyes adjusted. While she'd been in Nimue's grotto, the sun had risen. She heard men's shouts down by the river. At first she couldn't see Alba, and her stomach twisted with anxiety. Then there was a familiar whinny, and the mare trotted from the trees to meet her.

You have been ages! Bad men catch Evenstar again.

Rhianna's heart sank. She had taken too long. The Saxons had found her friend.

THE DARK
KNIGHT HAS
A NIGHTMARE

Mordred woke with a jolt. Something was wrong. Sweat bathed his whole body, and his stump throbbed.

He'd been having the old nightmare, where he was back on the battlefield duelling with King Arthur. Excalibur flashed down, slicing off his arm at the elbow. The bandages showed fresh blood where he must have knocked the wound in his sleep. But he'd become used to the pain, which usually faded when he woke up. This was different. Something had touched his spirit, exactly like when his Uncle Arthur had knighted him back in Camelot.

"No," he whispered. "No, it's not possible…" Fighting off the terror, he groped for his black mirror. "*Mother!*"

She appeared immediately, as if she'd been waiting for his call.

"I know, I felt it too. It seems Excalibur has been found."

"But the spirit magic! I thought you said it wouldn't work any more, now Arthur's dead—"

"Pull yourself together, boy!" his mother snapped. "It's your own fault for employing fools stupid enough to let a girl and a fairy with a harp get the better of them. So your cousin has got the sword out of the lake,

has she? That's good. Saves me the bother of dealing with Nimue. Don't worry.
The girl hasn't a clue how to use the spirit magic, and without Merlin to instruct her she won't find out. Or are you so feeble as to let a *damsel* command your knightly soul?"

Mordred's breath steadied. Now he thought about it, the touch on his spirit felt light and inexperienced, not firm and strong like his Uncle Arthur's. "Of course not," he said. "It was just a bad dream, that's all."

His mother sighed. "How many times do I have to tell you not to underestimate dreams? But there's no need to panic. There are a hundred Saxons between your cousin and Camelot. For now, let her think she has won. We'll let her and her friends tire themselves out fighting before we make our move."

Mordred prodded his tender stump and winced. "And what if the stupid fishmaid's enchanted the sword so it's no use to us any more?"

The witch gave an impatient hiss. "The Sword is one of the four Lights. No one can enchant it, not even me."

"But I thought you put a spell on it so I could kill Arthur?"

His mother laughed bitterly. "And a fine mess you made of that! You've been listening to too much squires' gossip. Do you think if I'd been able to spell the Sword of Light, you'd be a cripple with only one hand and I'd be stuck here in Annwn while your cousin wields Excalibur? Give me some credit. Be patient and it will help us too. Excalibur makes its own rules, and our brave Rhianna does not know them. I, however, have studied magic with the best. Remember what I taught you? Those who know the rules can always bend them."

Mordred felt a bit better. "Let me bend them for you, Mother," he said, clenching his good fist. "I'll teach my cousin to play with magic she doesn't understand."

"That's my boy," the witch said. "Now listen, this is what we're going to do…"

◄◙ 9 ◙►

Warrior Damsel

The power of Annwn grows ever strong
When winter grips the land so long
Grave are the dangers that lie in wait
To keep the friends from Camelot's gate.

At first, remembering the hut back in the Saxon camp and its smell of burned flesh, Rhianna didn't want to leave the warmth and safety of the enchanted lake. Then Alba sniffed at the sword, making it flare silver, and she heard a voice in her ear: "*Courage, daughter.*"

She looked round in sudden hope but saw only sunlight slanting through the trees. This must be a test, she decided, to see if she was worthy of carrying the Sword of Light. Perhaps her father's ghost was watching to see what she would do next? She smiled grimly. Things had changed since last time the Saxons had captured them. Pushing the mare's nose away, she quickly used her cloak to rub herself dry, then dragged on her armour over her wet sack-dress and vaulted into the saddle. She headed out of the trees gripping Excalibur tightly.

The Saxon boats seemed to be dredging the river, but their nets had become hopelessly tangled in the reeds. While their grumbling crews tried to sort out the mess, Rhianna cantered Alba down to the water's edge and galloped past them across the surface of the river in a silver spray. The men looked up when they heard the mare's splashing hooves and their mouths dropped open in disbelief. They were too surprised even to snatch up their weapons until she was safely past. Their oars tangled their nets still further as they tried to turn their boats to follow her.

"Did you just see a warrior maid riding over the water on a white horse…?" one said. "Nah, she's one of them water sprites," said another. "Leave her be, or she'll drown us all."

Rhianna was too worried about her friend to laugh. Where she'd left Elphin, only churned-up prints showed in the mud. The tracks led along the riverbank then turned into the wood. One of the horses had left small, unshod hoof prints in a broken trail – Evenstar, obviously misting. There were four larger horses and maybe two or three men on foot, she couldn't be sure. She urged Alba off the water and followed the prints, swinging Excalibur to clear the path.

She caught up with them sooner than she expected, rounding a bend in the track to see Evenstar being dragged along by his cursing captors. The little horse was not making it easy for the men, misting around tree trunks and tangling his reins. Elphin walked in the middle of the group with his hands bound and leashed to the leading rider's saddle. Rhianna's heart quickened as she saw the winged standard and recognised the bloodbeard captain who had tortured Sir Bors. Her friend's head was bowed and his dark curls tangled. She could see a bruise on his cheek and mud all down the front of his tunic where he must have been dragged along the ground.

Fury filled her. Digging her heels into Alba's sides, she raised Excalibur over her head and charged the men. "Duck, Elphin!" she yelled, slicing at the standard as she galloped past. Her blade cut the pole in half, and the eagle fell in the mud.

I fight too!

With an angry snort, the mare kicked out at Evenstar's captors, making them let go of the mist horse's reins. The men on foot flung themselves into the undergrowth to avoid being trampled. The horses threw up their heads, saw Rhianna galloping down upon them, with her copper hair frizzy from her swim and Excalibur flashing in the sunlight, and plunged off the path in alarm. Elphin eyed the swinging sword with disapproval. But he ducked as she'd warned him to, and her blade sliced through his leash, trailing silver light.

The bloodbeard captain dragged his horse round, his own sword scraping from his scabbard. But the blow that might have taken off her arm turned aside in midair, as if sliding off an invisible shield.

"*Excalibur!*" he said, his eyes widening.

It was enough for Rhianna to cut her friend's bonds. Elphin raced for his horse and vaulted into the saddle.

"Go, Rhia!" he yelled. "I'll follow and mist our trail."

But she was having too much fun. The sword gleamed around her and Alba, encasing them in a web of power that made her Avalonian armour shine and the air hum. Her whole body fizzed, bright and strong. She felt afraid of nothing, as if she led an army of her father's knights. The mare pranced, also unafraid, recognising the magic as something of Avalon. Within its protective light, Rhianna had time to see the bloodbeard's dismay as he recognised her. His men had regained control of their horses but seemed afraid to approach the glittering sword.

She laughed at their leader's expression. "Give my friend back his harp!" she ordered. "And while you're at it, you can give me back my father's shield, too. It belongs in Pendragon hands like this sword."

A sudden wariness appeared in the eyes of his men.

The bloodbeard captain had recovered from his surprise. His expression turned sly. "You're in no position to give orders, Pendragon maid. Or have you an army hiding in these woods, perhaps?" He glanced at the trees and chuckled. "Thought not. Prince Mordred's going to be very pleased with me. Not only have you saved us the bother of dredging all the lakes between here and the Summer Sea, but you've delivered yourself and Arthur's sword into our hands. I thought it strange when we captured you at Camelot, a damsel riding with knights all dressed up in your fancy armour. I'd never have left you with that fool Cynric if I'd known who you were. You won't escape again." His tone hardened. "Hand over Excalibur, and I'll tell my men to be gentle with you – or as gentle as they know how to be." He bared his teeth at her.

"Just you try to take it," Rhianna challenged him, remembering how Nimue had said the Sword of Light turned on its enemies and curious to see what would happen.

"Rhia!" Elphin choked, holding Evenstar back to wait for her. The men had regained their feet and drawn their swords, while the mounted bloodbeards went for their bows, their faces ugly. She had made them look stupid twice now, and they didn't like it.

Then their captain reached into his saddlebag and pulled out the grisly black hand he'd been using to torture Sir Bors back at the Saxon camp. Now Rhianna understood how he meant to take Excalibur to his master. The air around them darkened, and her wrist tingled in memory. The sword suddenly became heavier, dragging at her arm, and she heard the ominous flap of large wings approaching from the river. Coming to her senses at last, she wheeled Alba to join her friend. Together, they barged their way through all the bloodbeards and galloped into the trees.

She took the most difficult route she could, guiding Alba through the narrowest gaps between the trunks and under the lowest branches, seeking cover from the dragon as well as escape from Mordred's band. Behind her, she heard Elphin desperately humming under his breath as Evenstar misted. His yelps, as twigs whipped him, told her the magic did not work quite as well here in the land of men as it had back in Avalon. She smiled grimly, glad of all the practice she'd had. Even so, she caught several slaps in the eyes and lay flat over her mare's neck, swinging Excalibur blindly to cut a path. Her arm ached, and she was terrified one of the arrows hissing through the trees after them would hit her friend. But it worked. The men on foot couldn't catch them, the dragon couldn't see them through the dense leaves, and the bigger horses soon got left behind.

When the sounds of pursuit had faded, they drew rein, gasping for breath, and checked the sky.

Dark thing gone. Alba said in satisfaction. *I think we won.*

"Sorry," Elphin said. "I know I should have hidden when it got light, but then the bloodbeards turned up and I was afraid they might catch you at the lake. I managed to tangle the Saxons' nets with my harp, but my fingers…" He winced in memory. "The only thing I could think of was to let them capture me. But you were ages! What happened down there? I thought you'd drowned."

Rhianna hung over Alba's neck, too exhausted to answer. She thought of the nets and Saxons she had seen. "They'll be untangling that lot till next winter!" she said with a weak grin. "They wouldn't have found Excalibur, though. The lake spirit had taken it. I had a hard job persuading her to let me have it back. She said I mustn't blood the blade, or we can't take it back to Avalon. Is that true?"

Elphin eyed the glimmering sword in her hand. "Father did say something about keeping it clean... it makes sense. Blood interferes with our magic. Only those who work dark magic use blood in their spells. So you'd better remember not to kill anyone with it." He looked a bit relieved.

"She also said something about the hilt..." Rhianna shook her head. Nimue's words had unsettled her. She needed to ask Merlin about the spirit magic and find out why he'd really brought her here to find the sword. "Never mind. I got to Excalibur before Mordred, that's the main thing. Did you see those bloodbeards' faces? Even funnier than those Saxons', when Alba galloped past their boats on the river!"

Elphin eyed her bare feet and her wild cloud of tangled hair. "You were terrifying back there," he said in admiration. "For a moment I thought you did have an army hiding in the woods! You're—"

"Crazy. I know." Rhianna grinned at him again as she thought of how the bloodbeards had scattered. Then she remembered they still had her shield and Elphin's harp, and sobered. "We have to get our things back," she said.

"Not on our own," Elphin said. "There's dark magic in that arm. The bloodbeards can use it to contact Mordred somehow. If they've found out about you being Arthur's daughter that means Mordred knows as well. They'll be ready for you next time."

Rhianna knew he was right – surprise only worked once. "We'd better find Cai and the knights, I suppose," she said in a resigned tone. "Can you remember the way back?"

Elphin studied the trees and nodded. "I think so. But Rhia… there's something else you should know."

His tone worried her. She finished wiping Excalibur's blade on Alba's mane and looked up. "What?"

"Merlin. The bloodbeards told me Mordred's mother took his soul – they call her Morgan Le Fay because she's a witch. She's dead now, but apparently she made some kind of pact with the Lord of Annwn for her son's life, and she still advises Mordred from beyond the mists. Once you get close enough to the land of men, the mists can lead both ways, to Avalon or to Annwn. She must have ambushed Merlin while he was bringing us across. I should have realised when we saw that shadrake... I'm sorry. I know he was your father's friend."

"Merlin's gone to Annwn? Are you sure?" Rhianna gripped Excalibur tighter, thinking of the dream she'd had at the stone circle. The old druid might have tricked her about the sword bringing her father back to life, but he didn't deserve that.

"I don't know. Nobody with Avalonian blood can go to Annwn, but Merlin's half human, so his human soul would be vulnerable."

Rhianna stared at her friend in despair. "Then what about my dream? He told me to take Excalibur to Camelot and wait for him there. How are we supposed to get back to Avalon without him?" For a moment she couldn't think what to do next. Then she shook her head. "Those bloodbeards must have been lying. Merlin wouldn't let a witch overpower him. He was my father's druid, the most powerful magician in the land!"

Elphin sighed. "They might have been trying to scare me, I suppose. Or maybe Merlin found a way to escape. But if he's not at Camelot, we must find another way to get the sword back to Avalon as soon as we can. Only without Evenstar's shoes and something to open the mists, I'm not sure how." He bowed his head again so his curls shadowed his bruise. "I'm sorry, Rhia. I'm not much use to you, am I?"

"Don't be silly." She sat up straighter,

gathered up Alba's reins and took a deep breath. "I'd never even have got to the lake before Mordred's men without you. We're a team, just like King Arthur and Merlin… why are you looking at me like that? I won't make the same mistakes my father did." She hoped not, anyway. "Look, I've got Excalibur! We're both still free. And so are Cai and my father's knights, hopefully. If we can persuade them to chase that fat old Cynric and his Saxon bullies away from Camelot, we might be able to contact Merlin using the Round Table, like Sir Bors said. I just hope the knights aren't too angry with us—"

"They're furious!" said a voice from the undergrowth, making them both jump.

A plump figure, bristling with twigs and leaves, fought its way out of the bushes complaining loudly. Rhianna raised Excalibur. Elphin's hand went for his missing harp. But Alba pricked up her ears and snorted. *It is the human boy.*

"Did you have to ride into the thickest thicket this side of the river?" grumbled the green boy, picking leaves and twigs out of his hair. "We been looking for you ever since we woke up! Sir Bors says you're both foolish young hotheads who deserve to be whipped like errant squires, royalty or not... sorry, Damsel Rhianna. And by the way, we've got your shield back. Sir Agravaine says you'd best carry it next time you decide to take on a troop of Mordred's bloodbeards single-handedly."

Elphin smiled. "Try telling Rhia that. I think she enjoys scaring us."

Rhianna laughed in relief and slipped the

sword under her saddle flap so it wouldn't accidentally cut anyone. "Cai! Are we glad to see you. What took you so long?"

❧

Explaining breathlessly how they'd come across Mordred's broken standard and chased his scattered men through the wood, Cai led them back to the path, where they found the three knights with their rescued property. Two of Mordred's bloodbeards lay dead in the mud. Groaning on his knees at the sharp end of Sir Agravaine's lance, a third nursed a broken arm. The others, including the bloodbeard captain with the dark fist, must have got away.

Sir Bors looked to be fully recovered. He strode across to Rhianna and seized her by the arm. "You idiot girl! You little fool!

What did you think you were doing, going off alone like that?"

Furious tears sprang to Rhianna's eyes. She tried to tug out Excalibur to show him. But the big knight gripped her wrist and shook her hard.

"Never do that again!" His glare included Elphin.

"We rescued you from the Saxon camp!" Rhianna yelled back, her eyes flashing just as dangerously as the knight's. "If it hadn't been for us, you'd still be back there in the hands of Mordred's bloodbeards! Besides, you were asleep. We couldn't ask you to show us where you threw away the sword, could we?"

"She has a point, Bors," Sir Bedivere said, fighting a smile. "I did tell her to wait until you woke up, but you know the young. Impatient as always."

"You could have been killed," the knight said in a choked tone, unexpectedly putting his big arm around Rhianna and crushing her in an awkward hug. "Then what would I have told Merlin when he turns up?"

Rhianna eyed Elphin over his shoulder, wondering if any of them would ever see Merlin again.

Sir Bors let her go and examined her for damage. "By some miracle you seem to be in one piece," he muttered. "But from now on, I'm not letting you out of my sight. This…" he held up Elphin's harp bag, "… stays with me until we're safely inside the walls of Camelot."

Elphin did not look happy, but Rhianna guessed his fingers would not be up to playing much magic for a while, anyway.

"Elphin won't use it on you again, Sir Bors,"

she said sweetly. "He won't have to, not now I've got Excalibur."

Sir Bors went very still. The other two knights glanced at each other. Cai smiled. He'd seen the sword shining in the woods, but said nothing.

"How do you think I rescued Elphin from Mordred's men?" she said just as sweetly, wriggling out of Sir Bors' hug and lifting her saddle flap. Silver light shone across the path.

Sir Agravaine examined the sword, careful not to touch it. "It's Excalibur all right," he confirmed, looking at Rhianna differently.

Sir Bedivere smiled at her. "I thought those bloodbeards looked as if they'd seen a ghost. Well done, Damsel Rhianna."

Sir Bors blinked at her and shook himself. "Right," he grunted. "Wrap that sword back up, and get this piece of filth on a horse. We're taking the lot of you up to camp before anything else happens."

✦

As they rode, Rhianna straightened her armour over the sack-dress, which was at least cleaner after its dip in the lake, and tried to do something about her hair. This proved impossible without a brush. She settled for tying it into a frizzy ponytail with a length of ivy. She kept an eye on the trees, hoping for another glimpse of her father's ghost, but saw only small birds and squirrels.

Towards evening, they passed a sentry with a muttered password, and saw fires glimmering ahead of them in the dusk. Soon they made out the dark shapes of tents. Lines of tall, strong horses dozed nearby. They smelled smoke and roast boar, and heard men's voices interrupted by angry shouts as tussles broke out. At Sir Bors' command, two men dragged the prisoner off his horse and into a tent. "He might know where Mordred's hiding out," Sir Bors said. "Keep him alive."

When the prisoner had gone, Rhianna quietly strapped the dragon shield to her arm and untied the wrappings about Excalibur. She slipped the golden torque she'd stolen from the Saxon chief round her neck. Then she gathered up her loose reins and lifted her chin. "Look regal, Alba," she whispered.

I am too tired, the mare complained.

"So am I, but this is important. Do you want those stallions over there to think you're a scruffy Saxon pony?"

That did the trick. The little mare snorted, arched her neck and pranced obediently between the knights' big horses. Sir Bedivere waved to his friends in the camp, while Sir Agravaine glared about him with a surly expression. Several of the men called after Sir Bors, demanding to know what he'd done with King Arthur's body. Soon they had gathered quite a crowd, but they saw no women or girls. Battle-scarred men and a few older squires stared sullenly at Rhianna and the two mist horses.

"Who's the damsel, Bors?" someone called, and there were one or two wolf whistles from the older squires. Sir Bors kicked away a lad who tried to take Alba's rein. Elphin kept them away from her other side, his eyes purple and wary. Cai scowled dangerously at the boys in the crowd.

Rhianna clenched her jaw. She squeezed

Alba past the knights' big horses and trotted to the front. She raised Excalibur over her head until the flames of the campfires reflected in the blade and made the white jewel glow. A little of her energy returned, though nothing like as fiercely as when she'd attacked the bloodbeards in the wood.

"I am Rhianna Pendragon!" she announced in her loudest voice. "And this is my father's sword Excalibur, which the Lady of the Lake has given back to me!"

Silence fell over the clearing. The campfires crackled and spat sparks. Excalibur had brightened at the sound of her voice, but now looked like an ordinary sword again, its jewel dull in the gloom. People eyed it, muttering uneasily, "Can't be Excalibur... I thought only Arthur could carry the Sword of Light..."

until even Rhianna began to doubt the sword's magic. Her arm trembled with weariness, and she lowered the blade.

The men took this as a signal to grumble among themselves:

"*Who* did she say she was?"

"King Arthur's dead, he ain't coming back."

"We're finished. Nobody's goin' to drive the Saxons out now Arthur's gone."

"Mordred's lot will be in Camelot come spring. We were better off under the Roman eagle, if you ask me."

Rhianna clenched her fists. This wasn't what she had imagined at all. Where were the proud banners, flashing armour and glittering lances she'd seen in Merlin's song-pictures? These men looked like surly beaten villagers, not King Arthur's great knights.

"I *am* Rhianna Pendragon," she said again. "And my father is not dead. He's sleeping in Avalon, waiting for me to take him his sword so he can return to lead you all again."

The knights muttered uneasily. A few people laughed.

"Prove it," somebody called.

"Yeah, what are you up to, Bors? Trying to tell us this is some daughter of Arthur's? The king never had no daughter. We'd have known."

"Maybe we wouldn't, if Merlin had anything to do with it," someone muttered, but she couldn't see who had spoken.

"My mother's trapped in Camelot by the Saxons," Rhianna said, trying a new approach. "Even if you don't believe who I am, your queen needs you."

This raised another smattering of laughs.

"The queen don't need us!" someone said. "Not when she's got the brave Sir Lancelot to look after her."

Rhianna frowned. She wondered who Lancelot was, but there was no time to think about that now.

"Shut up, you fool!" hissed another. "That's Excalibur she's holding, all right. What if the girl really is Arthur's daughter? That means she's heir to the Pendragon throne, don't it?"

"She speaks the truth." Elphin rode his horse up beside Alba and spread his blistered fingers so they could all see the extra ones. "I am Prince Elphin of Avalon, and I can confirm Damsel Rhianna is King Arthur's daughter, brought to Avalon as a baby and raised there as my own sister." He put magic in his voice, but without his harp it did not reach very far through the suspicious crowd.

"The maid speaks the truth," Sir Bors growled, dismounting. "And anyone who don't believe it fights me, here and now!" He drew his sword. Sir Agravaine quickly planted his lance in the ground and joined him. Sir Bedivere, rolling his eyes in despair, drew his sword as well and stood with the other two knights.

Cai looked worried. "Please, Damsel Rhianna," he said. "Don't let 'em fight! Someone always gets hurt, and we squires are the ones who have to clean up after them."

Rhianna glanced at Elphin. He quietly freed his harp from Sir Bors' saddle. Wincing a bit, he strummed the strings. The Avalonian music rippled through the camp, making Excalibur shine again. The men at the front stood up straighter and smiled.

But Elphin's fingers were obviously still too sore to work the magic properly. He shook his head and said, "Sorry, Rhia. You'll have to think of something else."

Rhianna eyed his mist horse and had an idea. "Can I borrow Evenstar?"

Her friend gave her a puzzled look, but dismounted and passed her the reins.

She urged Alba into the thickest part of the crowd, leading Evenstar on a long rein beside her. As she'd hoped, Elphin's little horse misted a few times to avoid trampling people, making them blink and whisper uneasily.

"I'm sure my father wouldn't want you to kill each other," she said. "If any of you don't believe I can use Excalibur and was raised in Avalon, then they can mount my friend's horse and duel with me the Avalonian way." She held Excalibur in a fighting stance, hoping no one would take up her challenge or know enough about Lord Avallach's people to realise nobody ever duelled there. "Well?" she demanded. "Any of you brave knights want to call me a liar?"

A few of the men looked sideways at Evenstar and muttered about fairy horses and their tricks. Others dropped their hands towards their swords, but did not draw them. As the red light reflected in her blade, a ghost moved in the corner of Rhianna's eye. She couldn't risk turning her head to look at it, but she grinned. Her father had not abandoned her.

"Crazy girl's just like Arthur was as a boy!" a grizzled old knight muttered, breaking the tension. "Ready to fight us all, before he'd even had a day of training."

"She does have Excalibur, though!"

"And a prince of Avalon to do magic for her. Let's just hope he's better at it than old Merlin was… ah, what's the harm? I'll believe the maid is who she says she is till someone tells me different." He creaked down on one knee.

The others glanced at one another. "It's Excalibur we serve, isn't it?" someone else said, joining him. "I've not forgotten my oath to my king."

One by one, the knights bent their knees to Rhianna. She stared at their bowed heads, seeing their greasy, tangled hair, but also seeing muscles bulging in the firelight, battle scars, well-oiled swords, and the occasional glint of gold around their necks under their ragged tunics. These men were more than villagers in rusty armour. They had fought many battles with her father, and – if the songs were true –

won all except the last one against her cousin Mordred.

She felt a bit embarrassed. "Oh, please get up," she said. "I want you to fight the Saxons for me, not bow to me. King Arthur mightn't be here to lead you, but his spirit is still in this sword. You're going to win the next battle, I promise!" She reached for the stars with Excalibur, and the white jewel flamed with the energy of her voice.

It was the right thing to say. The knights cheered. Suddenly, men were slapping Sir Bors and Sir Agravaine and Sir Bedivere on the shoulders, congratulating the three knights on bringing Excalibur and Arthur's daughter back to them. Even Cai got his arm gripped by the other squires, who all wanted to know what it had been like in Fairyland. Cai went off happily to tell them wild stories over supper that Rhianna knew couldn't be true.

"*Well done, daughter,*" a voice said in her ear.

Though she couldn't see anything when she turned, a warm glow spread through her. It would be all right. As soon as they found Merlin they would take Excalibur back to Avalon, where it would be safe from Mordred until her father's body healed. Then they would return together to deal with the dark knight, and no one would be able to say she was not King Arthur's daughter.

She smiled to herself and went to unsaddle Alba.

⚜

After that, things got better. Rhianna slept for a whole day without dreaming, and woke to find a different camp. The men were training the older squires to fight with wooden swords, and there was much laughter as they set up a training target and tilted each other off the big horses with blunted lances. The younger squires whistled as they went about their work, slopping buckets and oiling armour, sharpening blades and clearing dung. Sir Bors found Rhianna some spare squires' clothing to replace her sack-dress. She especially liked the soft deerskin boots, which kept her feet dry and warm. The horses seemed in better spirits, too, munching nosebags of oats commandeered from nearby villages. Rhianna even managed to rescue a few apples for Alba before Cai ate them all.

She gave Elphin's bandaged hands a suspicious look, but he shook his head.

"It's all down to you," he explained. "I'm saving my songs for the victory feast at Camelot."

"They're going to fight, then?" Rhianna asked, her heart pounding.

"They'll fight." Elphin's eyes darkened to purple. "There isn't any other way in this world, apparently."

But to her frustration, they didn't set out for Camelot immediately. Sir Bors said they had to prepare properly. Many of the men were still recovering from wounds taken in the battle against Mordred's forces that had killed King Arthur. They had to find and train replacement horses. They were going to need anti-siege machines to use against the Saxon camp. Also, the knights and squires and horses had to be fed, and they all ate an incredible amount of food.

Rhianna tried to control her impatience.

After all, neither she nor Elphin knew anything about battles – and Cai didn't seem to know very much, either, in spite of his squire's training. But she knew she somehow had to learn how to use her father's sword before the battle, at least to defend herself and avoid blooding the blade.

After spending a few days watching the older squires bashing each other in the clearing set aside for training, she strode into the middle of them and drew Excalibur from the battered scabbard Sir Bors had given her.

"Teach me to fight!" she demanded.

They just laughed at her.

"Out of our way, Damsel!" called a lanky lad with curly brown hair. "Or you might get hurt."

"You'll get hurt, you mean!" Rhianna snapped, filled with a sudden dark anger.

Forcing him to defend himself, she caught his clumsy blow on Excalibur's blade. The magic sword smashed the wooden one into tiny pieces, and the squire yelled as a splinter went into his finger. He flushed as he sucked the wound.

The other boys crowded round, eyeing her glimmering sword warily. Too late, she remembered Lady Nimue's warning about blooding the blade and realised how stupid she was being. But she couldn't back down now. All she could do was try to keep the Sword of Light from cutting anyone before they let her go.

As she hesitated, another wooden blade struck her hand from behind, and Excalibur fell into the mud. She stared at it foolishly, the strange dark desire to fight them gone. The boys cheered and pressed closer, pulling her braid and prodding her with their wooden weapons, none too gently.

"Whack her, Gareth!" they called. "Teach her a lesson for blooding your finger!"

It was Rhianna's turn to flush. Nothing had changed. She was still the odd one out, the one they all teased because she was different. But none of them dared touch the sword she'd dropped.

Then Sir Bors was there. He shoved the boys aside, scowled at Rhianna and thrust a wooden blade into her hand. "If you want to learn to fight, my lady, then you do it the way everyone else does. Or the way they're meant to do it... ten to one are not fair odds, lads, are they? Even if you brave squires weren't fightin' a damsel."

The boys backed off, looking sheepish.

"But she was using Excalibur on us, sir," said Gareth, the boy whose sword she'd broken. "It might've eaten our souls!"

"And don't forget I drove off a troop of Mordred's bloodbeards on my own!" Rhianna said, raising her chin. "How many of your damsels can do *that*?"

The squires glanced sideways at her, as if they didn't know whether to believe her.

Sir Bors shook his head. "In King Arthur's camp, you learn to fight chivalrous, not dirty like the barbarians do. And that includes you, my lady. Right, you hold a sword like this... feet a bit wider apart... that's it. Now then, when he comes at you, you raise it up like so and—"

"Ow!" yelled Gareth as she struck him on the elbow, making him drop his replacement weapon. "Not fair, sir! She changed hands!"

Sir Bors smiled. "Left-handed, eh? That can be an advantage in a battle. The enemy don't expect it. Stop whining, boy, and let that be a lesson to you. Saxons have left hands, too, you know. And when you meet them, they won't be using wooden blades. Now then, again!"

By the time the lesson had finished, Rhianna was sweating as much as she had after rescuing Elphin from Mordred's men. Every muscle in her body ached, and her arm trembled from blocking the others' blows with the wooden sword. But she was grinning from ear to ear.

Sword fighting was very like dancing, really. You had to dance out of the way of your enemy's blade, while making a shield around yourself with your own that no blade could slip through. Easy enough for someone who had grown up in Avalon, where children learned to dance as soon as they could walk. And although Sir Bors gave her a ticking off afterwards for dropping Excalibur in the mud, her blood fizzed and her heart sang.

She would learn to be a great warrior! She would lead King Arthur's knights to Camelot and drive off the Saxons for him, and when he was reborn she would fight at his side against Mordred and his bloodbeards! Then her father would be proud of her, even though she was his daughter rather than his son. Rhianna Pendragon, the bravest damsel who ever lived…

Still grinning, she burst into the tent Sir Bors had given them, eager to tell her friends about her lesson. She found a nervous Cai peering under the mats and behind the curtains. "Lost something?" she said, thinking the boy must be after food of some sort, as usual.

Elphin's purple gaze silenced her. "Mordred's man is dead," he said. "A snake got into the tent where he was being kept and bit him. The men guarding him saw his body dissolve into green smoke. I think it was poison sent from Annwn so he wouldn't talk."

◁ 10 ▷

Shadrake

The Saxons trembled in dismay
When Arthur's knights rode out that day;
While alone beneath the dragon's wing
A damsel fought, bold as a king.

The snake had left a trail of ice from the dead prisoner's tent to the undergrowth, where it vanished into the night. If anyone doubted Elphin's word that it had been sent from Annwn, they soon changed their minds when a cold mist descended over the clearing, crackling in the bare branches of the trees and chilling everyone to the bone. But at least its attack spurred the camp into action.

The knights checked their weapons and ordered the squires to finish making repairs to their horses' harnesses. Fires were stoked up against the dark. Rhianna shivered herself to sleep under her fur with Excalibur beside her in its battered scabbard. She had a dream in which the sword whispered to her, daring her to draw it, and woke to find her hand gripping the hilt. She snatched it away uneasily. Elphin sat cross-legged at the tent flap. He'd been awake all night as far as she could tell, his harp resting in his lap between his bandaged hands.

In the morning they found three of the horses dead, their manes white with frost.

The mist horses were still safe, though Alba's coat was stiff with dried sweat under the sacking she wore against the cold. The little mare whinnied thankfully to Rhianna when she brought her breakfast in a nosebag.

Bad thing kill three stallions, Alba told her. *They fight bravely to protect us.*

"Poor mare!" Rhianna said, rubbing the cold white ears. "Why did I ever bring you out of Avalon? If that snake creature had bitten you, I'd never have forgiven myself."

"Mist horses can't die of Annwn's poison," Elphin said. "They were safe enough."

Rhianna scowled at her friend. "How do you know? You've never been in the land of men before, have you? You didn't even warn me it would be this *cold*!" Then she remembered him shivering at the tent flap all night, keeping watch, and felt bad. "It's all this waiting! What's the problem? Why don't they just get on and fight?"

Everyone was tense. Cai said it was only cold because it was winter, and complained that they would miss the midwinter feast if they didn't hurry up and get back into Camelot soon. Unable to believe the squire could think of his stomach at a time like this, Rhianna seized a wooden sword and worked off her energy fighting the squires in the training ring. Elphin watched her with purple-eyed disapproval, but said nothing. His hands were still bandaged, so there was no question of him holding a sword even if he had wanted to.

Finally, though, the preparations were done, and Sir Bors climbed on a log to address the men. He gave orders about transporting the siege equipment, and what the squires should do while the knights were away fighting at Camelot.

Rhianna's heart pounded with excitement. She brushed out Alba's tail until it crackled in the icy air. Then she pulled on her armour and hurried to fetch Excalibur and her shield. Amidst the buzz of the camp preparing for battle, nobody had time to notice her. Elphin stayed in the horse lines, talking softly to Evenstar.

"Where are you going, Damsel Rhianna?" Sir Bors said as their paths crossed. He had an armful of lances, which he added to a stack propped against an ancient oak. Cai and the other squires had the job of passing them out to the knights as they mounted up. The boy paused to wave at Rhianna, slipped on some ice and almost got himself trampled by an over-excited horse. He scrambled out of the way just in time, red-faced.

"I'm going to ride with you, of course!" Rhianna said.

Sir Bors shook his head. "You, damsel, are goin' to stay right here. I'm leaving a skeleton guard to look after you, and you've got Excalibur's magic to protect you so you should be safe enough. The younger squires'll stay with you. We need the older ones to fight."

"But I can fight too!" Rhianna could hardly believe he wasn't going to let her go with them. "I've been training."

The big knight smiled. "You've learned a few defensive moves. If any of them Saxons sneak in here when our backs are turned, you might need them. But until Camelot's back in our hands, you are staying right here where it's safe."

He dumped the lances and strode off.

"But it's not safe here! What if there are more of Mordred's bloodbeards creeping around? And what about that snake-thing…?" Rhianna called. But it was no good. The knights galloped off, led by Sir Bors, pennants snapping from their lances in the winter sunshine. They left Sir Bedivere in charge of the camp.

She eyed the knight they called Soft Hands, wondering what he'd do if she leaped on Alba and galloped after the others. He saw her expression and came over.

"I know it's not easy being left behind, Rhianna," he said. "But a battlefield's no place for the daughter of Arthur, believe me. We'll be there as soon as Bors sends word the castle's ours. You can lead the knights into Camelot, and you'll sleep in a proper bed tonight.

What would your mother think if she saw you get hurt in the battle?"

Rhianna supposed it wouldn't be very fair if, the first time her mother saw her, she was covered in mud and blood like her father had been in Merlin's boat the first time she saw him. Reluctantly, she unsaddled Alba, but the little mare made the job difficult by dancing around at the end of her reins and neighing after the other horses. *Not gallop with stallions?* Alba said with a disappointed snort.

"Not yet," Rhianna told her. "But you'll get your apples tonight, if all goes well. A warm stable, too."

Alba calmed down and shook her mane. *Good. This world is very cold and wet.*

Rhianna straightened the mare's rug and joined Cai and Elphin beside the glowing embers of their campfire. She eyed the trees, wondering if her father's ghost had gone with the knights. She hadn't seen it since their first night at camp, and hoped it wasn't angry with her for using Excalibur against the squires.

"What's the queen like?" she asked Cai. "Is she very beautiful?"

"I s'pose," the squire said.

"What about this knight who's supposed to be looking after her? Sir Lance-something?"

"Sir Lancelot's the greatest knight in all the land!" Cai told them, brightening. "He's King Arthur's champion and carries a magic lance. Least he used to, before he broke it."

Rhianna met Elphin's violet gaze, her heart quickening.

"Do you mean the Lance of Truth?"

she asked, thinking of Nimue's second riddle. *Who carries the Lance of Truth?*

Cai nodded. "I think Merlin used to call it that, yes. Dunno why."

Rhianna frowned. But she felt a bit better on hearing this news. If her mother had a champion knight looking after her, the Saxons were unlikely to hurt her even if the battle went badly.

"Sir Lancelot and my father must have been good friends if the king trusted him to look after my mother," she said.

"Er, not exactly," Cai mumbled, going red.

Rhianna would have liked to know more about her mother. But Cai seemed reluctant to speak of the queen. He kept changing the subject, telling them about the feast they held at midwinter to celebrate the Christ's mass, when King Arthur would knight all the squires who had completed three heroic deeds that year. Elphin wanted to know what qualified as a heroic deed, and the two boys got into an argument about whether killing someone in battle made you a hero or simply a murderer.

Rhianna poked the embers with Excalibur, thinking of the main reason they needed to get into Camelot. "Tell us how the Round Table works," she interrupted. "How did my father use it to contact Merlin?"

Cai pulled a face. "I dunno, do I? I told you before, we squires aren't allowed in there when the knights sit. But he used to take Excalibur in there with him, and it's a magic table, everyone knows that."

Elphin looked interested. "It might work

like Father's crystal palace back in Avalon. Maybe the sword wakes the magic in some way. What's the Round Table made of?"

"Stone, I think," Cai said.

"What sort of stone?"

"Dunno. Some kind of blue stuff. Merlin gave us a lesson about it once. It's supposed to be the same sort the ancients used to build their stone circles, something to do with the mists between worlds."

"That might be why you dreamed of Merlin at that circle we camped in," Elphin said, giving Rhianna a thoughtful look. "Did King Arthur only contact Merlin at the Round Table, Cai? Did he ever speak to anyone else using its magic?"

"He might have done... I wasn't really listening to tell you the truth. Merlin's a really grumpy teacher, and all that druid stuff about mists and spirit magic always makes my head spin. I'd much rather learn to joust."

Rhianna smiled. Jousting sounded fun. Maybe there would be time for her and Alba to learn after they got into Camelot. Then she sobered, remembering the Saxons and Mordred, and her father lying in Avalon waiting for her to bring him Excalibur to restore his strength. Until King Arthur sat on his throne again, they couldn't waste time enjoying themselves. "Could it have something to do with Excalibur feeding on souls?" she said.

Elphin frowned. "I'd forgotten that. But Merlin's a druid, so his soul wouldn't be trapped in the sword…"

As Elphin and Cai discussed swords and stones, it grew colder. She touched the jewel thoughtfully, remembering that Nimue had said the hilt was strong in spirit magic, but it felt no different. The clouds had thickened, and the pale morning faded to a gloomy winter's afternoon. It looked like rain again.

She began to worry. How long did a battle normally last? The daylight would be gone soon. Surely the knights wouldn't keep fighting in the dark? Did they stop for dinner and sleep, and start again the next day? She thought of the battlefield they'd seen, with the dead bodies and the ravens flapping their black wings.

Just as she felt certain Sir Bors had forgotten all about them and ridden into Camelot without her, a puffing Gareth galloped into camp on a pony dark with sweat, shouting, "Come quickly! Sir Bors says you got to bring Excalibur!"

Rhianna leaped to her feet and snatched up Alba's bridle.

"Slow down, lad!" Sir Bedivere told Gareth. "Breathe. Now tell us exactly what he said."

"Sir Bors said we need the magic sword at Camelot! The Saxons outnumber us, and there's this great big black dragon breathing ice everywhere and scaring all our horses!" The boy glanced nervously over his shoulder.

"The shadrake," Elphin said, his eyes turning purple.

Rhianna shivered. With all the excitement of the battle, she'd almost forgotten the dragon that was hunting them.

The knight thought for a moment. "There's no need for Damsel Rhianna to bring Excalibur. I'll send an escort with you," he continued to Gareth. "You should be able to handle the sword safely in its scabbard, if it's well wrapped."

"A lot of good that'll be!" Rhianna snapped, trembling with a mixture of excitement and fear. "I've got to go as well. No one else can use Excalibur, can they?"

Gareth rolled his eyes. Sir Bedivere looked at her doubtfully.

"That's true, sir," Elphin said. "The Sword of Light was forged in Avalon to serve those of the Pendragon blood. Its magic won't work for anyone else. I could handle it safely, maybe, but I couldn't use it against a dragon. My magic doesn't work properly when the shadrake's around, and my hands…" He lifted his bandaged fingers.

Sir Bedivere gave Rhianna another uncertain look. He didn't seem to know what to do. "Bors didn't ask for you as well, Damsel

Rhianna…" Finally, seeing her determined expression, he sighed. "All right. But you wear your armour at all times, you carry your father's shield, and you stay well away from the fighting. Elphin, you'd better come too. We'll need any magic you can manage."

"And me!" Cai said, pale but determined. "I can ride by myself now – ask Rhianna!"

Rhianna nodded, though her mouth had gone dry. She thought of Lady Nimue's warning about not getting blood on the blade, and the way the sword had made her forget this when she'd drawn it against the squires. In spite of Elphin's confident talk, she didn't have the first idea how to use Excalibur's magic against a dragon.

The sky darkened still further, and a few feathery white flakes whirled between the trees.

Sir Bedivere sighed and eyed the clouds. "That's all we need," he muttered. "It's far too late in the year for battles. Let's get going, before the snow comes."

❦

They heard the noise of the battle before they saw it. The ditches around Camelot were a struggling mass of men, trapped between the high white walls on one side and Arthur's knights on the other. The snow was coming down quite thickly now, melting as it landed and turning the mud into a slippery slush. The horses could not manoeuvre very well in the ditches, but the knights' long lances caught anyone who tried to escape by scrambling out. Sir Bors had set up his anti-siege machines around the outer ditch to rain missiles on the

Saxon tents. Meanwhile, the trapped defenders inside Camelot were throwing whatever they had – spears, stones, rotten fruit, dented cook pots – at any Saxons who tried to take shelter under the walls.

Sir Bedivere halted them on top of a small hill a safe distance away, where they peered through the whirling snow, trying to see who was winning. Elphin pressed his lips together at the sight of all the slaughter, his eyes purple with disapproval. But Cai punched the air with his fist and yelled, "Yah! Got him!" whenever one of the knights lanced a fleeing Saxon. Rhianna saw the boys she'd trained against crouched under a rock at the edge of the field, and felt guilty. They were not fighting with wooden swords today.

The Saxons might have been trapped, but the

knights seemed reluctant to ride down into the camp and meet their enemy. They could see why. The dragon Gareth had warned them of swooped over the walls of Camelot, making the defenders duck, its great wings shadowing Saxon and Briton alike. Rhianna recognised it at once as the creature that had attacked them at the Lonely Tor, though it seemed more solid in the daylight. Snow lay on its back, turning its black scales white. Rings and torques and jewelled daggers it had stolen from the dead glittered in a bulging pouch between its forelegs. With every dive its scaly tail lashed the knights below. Several horses whipped round and bolted. The Saxons ducked and made signs against evil after it, while ravens gave chase cawing in anger.

Those stallions are cowards, Alba observed. *I would not run away like that.*

Hoping the mare wouldn't mist instead, Rhianna dragged Excalibur from its scabbard. At once, the enchanted blade gleamed silver in the snow light. The white jewel on its hilt brightened, and the rush of power along her arm felt even stronger now than in the wood when she'd rescued Elphin from the bloodbeards. The strength of a hundred men? She'd soon find out.

"Over here!" she yelled. "Here I am!"

The creature's red eye fixed on the sword. It gave a triumphant shriek and flapped through the storm towards her with its mighty forelegs out-stretched. She raised the shield just in time to stop them knocking her out of the saddle. The blow made her arm vibrate, and she nearly dropped Excalibur.

"Rhia!" Elphin yelled as Evenstar misted to escape. "Don't let it breathe on you!"

Easier said than done.

Another blast of icy breath crackled over her shield to melt on her Avalonian armour. Vaguely, she was aware of Sir Bedivere shouting at his men to surround the hill with their lances to keep the Saxons at bay. She saw Cai helping Elphin to pull his harp out of its bag. Then Alba bucked and plunged down the slope, and the two of them were alone in the whirling snow with the dragon's black wings beating overhead.

Hoping the Avalonian armour would protect her, she undid the straps of the Pendragon shield with her teeth and cast it to the ground. Now she could swing Excalibur more easily. But she had not trained with a sword on horseback, and she could barely see through the storm. She hesitated to stab the shadrake in the belly.

Did creatures of Annwn bleed?

"I HAVE FOUND YOU, PENDRAGON," roared the creature, sounding pleased with itself. It dived at Alba again, making the mare spin round in panic.

They galloped around the other side of the hill with the dragon in pursuit. Excalibur brightened still further, and the snow around them thickened. Rhianna slowed Alba, afraid the mare would gallop into a ditch, and heard the shadrake flapping towards them again. She lay flat against Alba's neck as the creature's great wings brushed her hair then swept on past. A shudder went through her. That had been too close.

While she was looking to see where the shadrake had gone and wondering why it had not tried to kill her yet, a dark figure loomed out of the storm in front of them and a hand closed about her ankle. She felt Alba begin to mist and kicked frantically as a familiar face appeared out of the blizzard with frost in his beard and blue spirals on his cheeks. The bloodbeard captain.

"Got you now, Pendragon maid!" He bared his teeth at her as he pulled her off the misting horse.

Rhianna rolled out of his grip and sprang to her feet, instinctively bringing Excalibur up between them. He didn't seem to have a weapon, instead he brandished the black gauntlet he'd used to torture Sir Bors. Behind him stood the shadowy figure in black armour she'd seen in the hut. Her arm trembled. She could no longer seem to control her sword. It was as if an invisible hand had hold of her wrist. Excalibur's jewel darkened, the hilt twisted in her grip, and the blade flashed towards her enemy's exposed throat...

Then she heard the first notes of Elphin's harp, thin and wild across the battlefield. A hole appeared in the clouds and crimson sunlight stabbed across the hill.

"*Allow me, daughter.*" Suddenly, her father's ghost was there. Beside him stood another ghost, and beside him another... a whole army of ghostly knights, bathed in the red light.

King Arthur's ghost leaped at the dark knight and wrestled him to the ground. The noise of the fighting faded, and Rhianna's heart lurched in anxiety. Her father did not even have a helmet, although of course such things would be of no use to a ghost. In any case, she had other things to worry about.

Even as she watched the ghostly battle,

the shadrake lurched towards her again. This time it swerved around her, and its claw clouted the bloodbeard on the side of his head, knocking him through the air. Coming to her senses, she checked her swing just in time to avoid touching the man with her blade as he fell senseless at her feet. The black gauntlet rolled out of his hand, and the dark knight's shadow vanished in a glitter of black stars.

"You don't trick me that way!" Rhianna yelled, kicking the horrid fist away. Attracted by the glittering ring on the gloved finger, the shadrake chased after it and snatched the thing up to add to its pouch.

The clouds parted further, and Alba trotted back down the hill.

I am sorry I misted! the mare said. *Has the dragon gone?*

"Not yet," Rhianna answered through gritted teeth, catching the reins. "But I don't think it's trying to kill us. It must want something else. Be brave."

As the evening sun blazed across the battlefield, making men fling up their arms to protect their eyes, the shadrake swooped once more. She vaulted back on Alba and galloped up the hill to meet it. She flashed Excalibur through the air, faster and faster, enjoying the feel of the sword's power rushing along her arm. A great energy filled her, and she no longer felt afraid of the dragon, which was now being dive-bombed by a whole flock of birds angry that it had invaded their territory.

"What do you want?" she shouted. "You're scaring the horses."

Lightning crackled around the creature.

Was it her imagination, or did it laugh? "I HAVE SOMETHING FOR YOU, PENDRAGON."

It reached a claw into its pouch, and Rhianna stiffened.

"Then hurry up and give it to me, and go back to Annwn!" she ordered.

She ducked as the dragon somersaulted to avoid a final attack by a brave little hawk, spraying her with a glittering rain of treasure from its pouch. A pale thread glimmered from its mouth and twisted about the poor hawk, tumbling the little bird through the air. The shadrake shrieked one last time and faded, until all she could see was an outline of the snow on its back, pink against the clouds. Finally it was gone, leaving coins and jewels glittering over the Saxon camp as it vanished into the mists.

There came a smell of something rotten that made Rhianna choke and spit. Then the evening sun bathed her and Alba in glorious red and gold, and the foulness blew away.

Gaining new heart when they saw her on the hill with Excalibur, the knights re-formed their lines and charged the Saxon camp, making short work of the defenders. It was soon over. A horn sounded from the wall. The gates of Camelot opened, and a troop of old men and boys trotted out, behind a ragged banner with a red dragon rippling across a golden background in the breeze. At the sight of the banner, the knights gave a cheer and the Saxons – seeing they were beaten – began to surrender their weapons.

"Bravely fought, daughter," whispered a voice in her ear.

Rhianna grinned in pride. Something silver-bright had caught on the end of her sword, making it shine even more brilliantly. "We showed them, didn't we, Father?" she said, certain this time he'd be there when she turned.

But the ghost had already vanished into the sun.

While her father's knights took charge of the field, Rhianna checked Alba for injuries, relieved to find the mare unscathed. Now the shadrake had gone, so had her magical strength. She started to shake the silver thing off Excalibur and recognised the druid spiral from the end of Merlin's staff. Too tired to think about what that might mean, she slipped it into her pocket as the others gathered round to congratulate her.

"Is that Sir Lancelot?" she asked, squinting into the sun. None of the newcomers looked much like a champion knight to her. The lad holding the dragon standard seemed even younger than Cai.

Sir Bedivere frowned. "No. Those are the half-trained youngsters and pensioned-off knights King Arthur wouldn't take into battle. But they've done a good job holding the walls against the Saxons so long. This is a day for bravery from unexpected quarters, it seems. Camelot's ours, but I wouldn't get your hopes up too much for the queen."

He had no time to explain. Sir Bors and Sir Agravaine rode up, accompanied by Chief Cynric riding a Saxon pony. Rhianna stiffened,

not sure she had the strength for more fighting.
But the big Saxon chief had been disarmed.
One of his yellow braids had come unravelled,
and blood smudged his cheek. His men, also
weaponless, stood nearby in a muttering group.
The knights poked them with their lances and
told them to shut up.

"Princess Rhianna, Chief Cynric would like
to surrender Camelot to you," Sir Bors said,
looking very pleased with himself.

Alba was no smaller than his pony, but the
Saxon chief could still look down at her.
At least it was better than kneeling before him
wearing a slave collar. Rhianna summoned the
last of her energy, sat up straight in her saddle
and met the big man's gaze.

He saw the sword in her hand. Then his
eyes focused on her throat. Recognising the

gold torque she'd stolen from him, he blinked and looked closer at her face. "The slave maid," he whispered.

She smiled. Now he would find out how it felt.

"On your knees, barbarian!" muttered Sir Bors, pushing Cynric off the pony. He poked his sword into the chieftain's neck to make sure he obeyed.

The other prisoners muttered in disapproval, and Cynric gave the knight a fierce look. "I am a king among my people," he protested. "You have no right to make me kneel in the snow like a slave."

Sir Bors raised an eyebrow at Rhianna. "I hear you made Princess Rhianna kneel before you in a slave collar."

"Yes, he did!" Rhianna's voice carried across

the hillside. "And you also put a collar on my friend Elphin here, who is a prince of his people. But it's not right to make anyone into a slave, not even a humble squire."

"You tell him, Damsel Rhianna!" Cai called. "I still got blisters on my neck."

"Hush, Cai," Sir Bors said. "Princess Rhianna, do you want this barbarian scum kept alive to work the mines down in Lyonesse, or should I just kill him now and have done with it?"

Cynric glared at him. "I am not afraid to die, Briton!"

Rhianna eyed the big chief, wondering what her father would have done. Then she remembered how the Saxon had stopped the bloodbeard hurting her when she'd been a prisoner in his camp. "Let him stand," she said.

Sir Bors gave her a quick look. But he let the big man get up. Cynric looked at Rhianna with wary surprise.

She took the torque from around her neck. "I have something that belongs to you," she said. "It doesn't fit me very well, really. And you have something that belongs to me."

Cynric frowned. "But you took all your stuff when that magician boy sang my camp to sleep," he growled, glancing at Elphin.

"Sang my camp to sleep, *Princess*," Sir Bors corrected, giving the chieftain a prod in the back with his blade. "Rhianna is of royal blood. Remember who you are talking to."

Cynric scowled. "Then she should be addressed as Pendragon," he said defiantly. "If she's the daughter of Arthur like you claim." He eyed Rhianna, encouraged by her smile.

"My life is in your hands, Pendragon maid. If you let my men live, I'll make sure Saxons no longer fight Prince Mordred's battles for him."

Rhianna looked to the walls of Camelot, but her father's ghost gave her no clues. "I'll let your men live if you'll help us rebuild all those villages you burned," she said in the end. "And I'll give you your necklace back, if you give me the shoes your men stole from my friend's horse."

Elphin smiled too. But Cai looked confused. "Good gold for a few old horseshoes?" he grumbled. "Is she crazy?"

But Cynric gave Rhianna a look of respect. So did the other prisoners, as well as the knights guarding them. The chief nodded to his men. One of them sullenly undid his belt and slipped off four dainty silver shoes, tied together with a loop of twine. Elphin's face brightened. He whispered something to Cai, who marched across to snatch the horseshoes from the Saxon.

In return, Rhianna passed the chief his torque, and he twisted it back round his neck. He straightened a little and seemed to grow taller. "My men are tired of fighting. When we've helped you rebuild the villages, will you let us stay and raise our youngsters alongside yours?"

Sir Agravaine scowled. "Saxons in our villages? Do you think we were born yesterday?"

"It's not a bad idea," Sir Bedivere said with a little cough. "We'll be able to keep an eye on them there, and their children can join the squire school when they're old enough – train as knights to replace the ones we lost with Arthur."

"We'll want hostages for your good

behaviour in future," Sir Bors added quickly.

Cynric nodded. "Agreed."

Rhianna couldn't help feeling a bit sorry for the chief. "Give him his weapons back, too," she ordered.

"I'm not sure that's wise, Damsel Rhianna," Sir Bors muttered. "I wouldn't trust the barbarian no further than my horse could kick him. Best just chuck the Saxon scum out into the snow and keep their weapons. Remember what they did to me."

Rhianna didn't think she'd ever forget. "Are any of Mordred's bloodbeards still alive?" she said, shivering a little. "If so, they and the men who helped them can stay as our hostages."

Sir Bors nodded. But it turned out the remaining bloodbeards had fled when they saw their captain fall. The Saxons who had helped them torture Sir Bors were thrust forward, identified by their own comrades. They bared their teeth at Rhianna as Sir Agravaine ordered his men to strip them of their furs, remove their boots and take them away. Their pale bodies broke out in goosebumps as they hobbled through the snow.

Cynric made no protest. He raised his fist to his forehead. "You are your father's daughter, Rhianna Pendragon." With great dignity, he led the rest of his men from the battlefield, escorted by the knights, who would give them their weapons once they were a safe distance from Camelot.

Rhianna watched them go and finally sheathed Excalibur. All the remaining strength ran out of her. She closed her eyes and rested her forehead against Alba's damp mane. Even the cheering knights and the blowing horns, and the thought of meeting her mother at last, could not rouse a spark of energy. She'd used it all up fighting the dragon and dealing with the Saxon chief, which had been almost as tiring as the battle.

She did get to lead the knights victoriously into Camelot, as Sir Bedivere had promised. But it might as well have been a dream. Her head did not seem to belong to her body. Alba's hooves pranced soundlessly through the snow, and the mist horse's mane drifted like a pink cloud in the setting sun. The high walls towered above her, and the great arched gateway reared so far overhead it could have belonged to a castle in the sky. Only Elphin and Cai, riding close on each side to keep her in her saddle, seemed real.

"Is my father coming, too?" she whispered,

twisting her head to look for his ghost.

Her friends glanced at each other. "No, Rhia," Elphin said gently. "King Arthur's still sleeping in Avalon, remember? But we'll be back there soon."

"Make way for the Pendragon!" Cai yelled to the cheering people lining the streets, and the cheers got louder. People threw white winter roses that caught in Alba's mane. Rhianna didn't know if they were cheering her or the tattered Pendragon banner that rippled before her eyes until the red dragon seemed alive.

She fixed her eyes on it and wondered if her mother would recognise her. That was her last thought before welcoming hands pulled her off Alba's back and carried her up a winding stair to bed. She was asleep before her head touched the pillow.

Mordred Makes a Mistake

Tired of watching his cousin ride triumphantly into Camelot behind the Pendragon banner, Mordred threw the mirror to the floor in rage. Pain stabbed his arm, making him curl up on his rocky bed and clutch at his stump.

His men had failed! Not only had they allowed his cousin to take Excalibur from under their noses, but she had somehow used the sword to persuade Arthur's knights to fight. And now she was inside Camelot where his men couldn't reach her. He could sense her new strength even from his sanctuary. He'd tried to send his shadow to the battlefield to make her drop the sword so his bloodbeard could grab it, but something had blocked him. If he didn't know better, he'd have said it was his Uncle Arthur. Worse, the stupid shadrake had taken his fist, which meant he couldn't even contact his men until he got out of here... and he *hated* dragons.

"Stop being such a baby," his mother's voice came from the floor, faint but commanding. "Pick up that mirror and talk to me! We have to make new plans."

The last thing Mordred felt like doing right now was facing his mother. But the pain frightened him, so he obediently reached over the side of his bed and peered into the dark glass.

"My stump hurts," he complained. "Your stupid shadrake stole my fist." He wondered if his mother had told the creature to take his missing hand into Annwn to punish him for his men's failure. He wouldn't have been surprised.

"I didn't send the shadrake to Camelot, silly boy," the witch said. "It's been flapping around in the world of men like some overgrown bird ever since it snatched the druid's pathfinder as he came through the mists. Merlin must have managed the spirit transfer, after all – promised it treasure, I expect. But it's back here now and it's brought your fist, so it might still be of some use to us. In the meantime, we must stop Arthur's daughter taking the sword back to Avalon until you're well enough to get it

off her. The easiest way will be to trick her
into blooding it. She's stronger than we
thought, but she's bound to try using the
Round Table to contact Merlin, and she won't
be expecting trouble among her friends in
Camelot. Be ready when she calls."

Mordred sat up, interested. "Can I reach
her without my fist?"

"You still share your knightly link with
Excalibur. It's dangerous because you're not
the only one the sword knighted, but she
should be able to see and hear you all right."

"I'm not sure I want her to see me like
this." Mordred scowled at his stump, thinking
of his athletic cousin swinging Excalibur in
the battle against the dragon. He didn't want
her to think he was some kind of cripple.

"Have I made you vain, my son?" His

mother smiled. "You don't really understand the spirit magic, do you?"

"If you'd explain it a bit better, I might," Mordred muttered.

"No need to sulk. You were young when you sat at the Round Table. Don't worry, our fair damsel will see my handsome boy. Who knows, she might even fall for you. That'd be an interesting turn of events."

"Stop it, Mother!" Mordred said, alarmed now.

The witch laughed. "Don't look so worried. She was raised in Avalon remember? The girl's innocent enough to charm a unicorn. You concentrate on making her angry enough to draw Excalibur. Leave the magic to me."

◀◧ 11 ◨▶

Round Table

Ringed by Camelot's mighty wall
A table round to seat them all.
Where kiss of an enchanted sword
Did rouse the ghosts of ancient lords.

A beautiful lady with hair like flames bent over Rhianna's bed. A golden circlet glittered on her brow in the candlelight. Her eyes crinkled at the corners when she smiled.

Rhianna sighed in pleasure. "Mother?" she whispered.

"Go back to sleep, child." The lady kissed her on the forehead and straightened her fur coverlet. "You're safe now."

Rhianna drifted into a dream where her father came trotting out of the mists on one of Lord Avallach's horses, healed of his wounds and wearing a golden crown set with fiery jewels. She rode out to meet him with Excalibur, and her mother rode behind her with the champion knight, Lancelot, who looked handsome and young. The king smiled when he saw them and reached out his arms to Rhianna. But a shadow loomed between them, and when it turned she recognised the dark knight. He held something that shone so brightly she could no longer see the path.

"You're too late," he said. "Camelot is mine."

Then the light struck her eyelids, and she woke with a start.

The first thing she saw was a star framed by an arched window. The sky was a deep, velvety blue. In the grate a fire crackled quietly, scented with pine cones. She no longer wore her borrowed squire's clothing, but a soft white nightgown. A mattress cradled her tired body and furs lay heavy and warm over her legs.

For a moment she couldn't think where she was. Then her arm slipped out from under the covers and her hand touched cold stone. All at once, she remembered the battle and the dragon and her father's ghost fighting the dark knight's shadow. She sat up, clutching the furs to her chin, and looked with pounding heart for Excalibur.

With some relief, she saw the sword, safe in its battered scabbard, resting across her neatly folded cloak at the end of her bed. Her Avalonian armour glimmered beside it, also neatly folded. Merlin's spiral sat on top of the pile. She stared at the druid symbol, recalling her dream at the stone circle. *If all else fails, I'll send you my pathfinder… Look for the dragon.* The spiral must be his pathfinder, she supposed. Had Merlin sent that dragon after them? If so, she'd have something to say to him for scaring them like that.

She gazed curiously around the room. Curtains embroidered with gold and silver threads covered the walls, showing unicorns and dragons, and knights jousting with long lances. She was about to climb out of bed for a closer look, when she realised she was not alone.

A strange girl dozed on a stool near the fireplace.

"Who are you?" she said, alarmed.

The girl started awake and came hurrying over to the bed. "My lady, I'm sorry! I didn't mean to fall asleep. My name's Arianrhod. Lady Isabel says I'm to be your maid now." She tugged at the furs in an effort to straighten them. Black hair shadowed a thin, pale face. Rhianna felt a pang of disappointment that it wasn't her mother.

"Where's my friend Elphin, the Avalonian boy?" she asked. "And Cai?"

"Sleeping in the squires' dormitory, my lady," the girl said, keeping her face hidden behind her hair. "Damsels aren't allowed in there. The men celebrated after the Saxons left, drank a lot of mead. Sir Bors told me to stay with you until you woke up. You've slept for a whole day! It's nearly midnight."

"What about the queen? Is she asleep, too?"

"Er, no, my lady." Arianrhod twisted a fold of her dress between her fingers. "At least, I suppose she might be sleeping, but she's gone north with Sir Lancelot and his men. They left soon after we heard Prince Mordred had wounded King Arthur. Sir Lancelot said he was taking her to safety, a secret location. I thought you knew…" Her voice grew fainter, and she cringed as if afraid of being hit.

Rhianna sighed. So that was what the knights had been sniggering about back at the camp? "My mother's not here," she said, feeling hollow inside. She hadn't realised how much she had been looking forward to meeting the woman who had held her in her arms as a baby.

"No, my lady, I'm sorry. I'm sure she would

have stayed, if she had known you were coming. But up until yesterday none of us knew you even existed!"

"Who undressed me?" Rhianna asked, a bit embarrassed.

"Lady Isabel, of course. She's in charge of the Damsel Tower. I helped her put you to bed. I washed your hair, too. It's a really pretty colour, like autumn leaves." The girl gave her a shy smile. "It was very dirty. I had to cut some of the tangles out. I hope you don't mind."

Rhianna lifted a hand to her head and realised why it felt so light. Half her hair had gone. The rest had been bound into some kind of net. She tugged the thing off and flung it on the bed in a glitter of gold and tiny emeralds. "Never touch my hair again!" she said, unsettled by the thought of a blade that close to her head while she slept.

Arianrhod cringed again. "B-but Lady Isabel said I was to clean you up and make you look presentable…"

"Do you know who I am?"

"Yes, Princess Rhianna. You're Queen Guinevere's daughter."

"I'm Rhianna *Pendragon*, King Arthur's daughter," Rhianna corrected. "Didn't you see me in the battle?"

The girl eyed her warily. "We saw a great hero on a white horse fighting the dragon," she whispered. "Everyone said it was King Arthur come back from Fairyland to save us."

So she hadn't been imagining things. Other people could see her father's ghost, too.

"That was me on the white horse, silly!" Rhianna said fighting a smile. "Didn't you see Excalibur?"

Arianrhod nodded. "I thought it must be King Arthur's famous sword, because it gleamed so bright. That proves he came back to help us. Only King Arthur can use Excalibur without losing his soul."

Rhianna reached for the scabbard and freed the sword. The white jewel glittered in the firelight as she showed it to Arianrhod. "Recognise this, then?"

She didn't mean to scare her. An Avalonian girl would have laughed and flicked the weapon away with magic. But Arianrhod gave a little scream and huddled against the fireplace. "Please lady, don't cut me!"

As the black hair parted, Rhianna glimpsed a purple scar in the shape of a five-pointed star on the girl's cheek. Coming to her senses, she sheathed the sword and laid it back on the chest. She wanted to ask about the scar, but Arianrhod quickly pulled her hair back over it. In any case she had more important things to think about first.

"This sword is Excalibur," she said more gently. "And I did fight the dragon you saw out there – though there was magic involved, so I'm not surprised you saw King Arthur's ghost... I don't suppose you happened to see where he went after the battle?"

Arianrhod shook her head. "He just vanished. Went back to Fairyland, I expect."

"What about Merlin? We're supposed to be meeting him at Camelot. Is he here?"

Arianrhod shook her head again. "Nobody's seen Merlin since Prince Mordred killed the king."

Rhianna sighed. It had been too much to

hope that the druid would be here waiting for them. She straightened her shoulders. If she wanted to try magic to contact Merlin, now seemed as good a time as any. "Where's the Round Table?"

"Where it always was, my lady. In the Great Hall."

"Take me there."

Arianrhod met her gaze for the first time, surprise in her dark eyes. "Now? But it's the middle of the night... no one will be there."

Rhianna grinned as she pulled on her cloak and buckled Excalibur's scabbard over the white dress. "That's the whole idea, and please stop calling me 'my lady'. It's making me feel old. My friends call me Rhia."

On their way down the shadowed staircases and along the torchlit corridors of the sleeping castle, she discovered how Arianrhod had come to Camelot as a baby after being abandoned in the woods and found by Arthur's knights on a hunting trip. The king's sister, Lady Morgan, was living in Camelot at the time. She had no husband, just her small son Mordred – a quiet, dark-haired boy who was bullied by the other squires. People assumed Mordred's father had been killed in battle and felt sorry for his beautiful young mother. At first Arianrhod thought she'd enjoy looking after her. But she soon found out that none of Lady Morgan's maids lasted very long.

"I was only nine when she chose me," Arianrhod told her. "I had no idea she was a witch. Then Mordred got made a knight, and he and King Arthur had a big argument one day across the Round Table. Prince Mordred galloped off with the men who'd come down from the north to train at Camelot, and that night Lady Morgan took me to her rooms. She said she wanted me to help her make a spell. She made me drink something bitter that made me feel really strange. Then she called on the forces of Annwn and cut my cheek with a horrid black dagger. I don't know what happened after that. When I woke up, she had gone. She went off to be with her son, of course. The guards had orders to stop her, but they never saw her pass the gates. Some people say she sprouted wings like a bird and flew over the wall." She shuddered. "I hope she never comes back."

"She won't be back," Rhianna said, chilled.

"You don't need to be afraid of her any more, because she's dead."

"Lady Morgan's dead? Really?" Arianrhod touched her scarred cheek.

"Yes," Rhianna said firmly. "She's in Annwn, so she can never hurt you again."

At least she hoped Elphin was right about that, because she didn't fancy meeting a witch's ghost in these corridors.

They met several sets of sentries on their way to the Great Hall, who relaxed when they saw the two damsels. One man asked where they were going in the middle of the night. Arianrhod, who had cheered up a bit since learning of Lady Morgan's fate, winked at Rhianna and mumbled something about a midnight feast in the squires' dormitory. The sentry chuckled and warned them not to let

Lady Isabel catch them. None of them seemed to recognise Rhianna. She kept Excalibur hidden under her cloak and tried to control her impatience. All she'd found to wear on her feet was a pair of embroidered slippers. *I must look ridiculous*, she thought.

At last Arianrhod pulled her towards two enormous carved doors. Rhianna winced at the thought of the noise they would make as they opened. But Arianrhod produced a key and opened a little door in one of the larger ones. "We have to get in here to clean the place after the knights have been sitting," she explained as Rhianna ducked through.

Inside, Rhianna paused, the hairs on the back of her neck lifting. The lamp Arianrhod carried did not reach very far in the enormous room, but she could sense something huge and powerful humming in the shadows. The roof arched high overhead, reminding her of Lord Avallach's palace. Stars showed through a circular opening in the centre. The floor had a pattern of coloured tiles, like those she'd glimpsed under the weeds in the ruined Roman villa. Drawn up around the table were large stone chairs with velvet cushions on the seats.

She walked slowly around the chairs, touching their carved backs with her fingertips, wondering how the magic worked.

"My lad— I mean, Rhia… your sword!"

Excalibur's white jewel shone, warm against her leg. She drew the blade and at once it blazed silver, making Arianrhod look nervously at the doors.

At least they could see now. Holding Excalibur aloft like a torch, Rhianna completed her walk around the table, counting the chairs as she went. But when she reached the doors again, she found she had lost count. She shook her head, thinking of what Cai had said about Merlin enchanting the Round Table, so it would seat all the knights who wanted to talk with the king.

"Do you know how King Arthur used this table to speak to Merlin?" she asked Arianrhod.

The girl shook her head. "I'm sorry. Damsels aren't allowed in here when the knights meet."

"Like you're not allowed in the squire's dormitory?" Rhianna said with a grin.

"That's different," Arianrhod said, blushing.

Since all the seats looked the same, it probably didn't matter which one she chose. She marched up to the nearest and sat in it. Her feet did not reach the floor.

"I don't think you should sit there, my lady," Arianrhod whispered, glancing at the doors again.

Rhianna rested Excalibur on the table in front of her, imagining the knights seated around her. Cai had been right about the table being made of blue stone. Spirals had been carved into it, which shifted and glimmered in the light of her sword. She stood on the chair to see them better.

"Rhia!" Arianrhod hissed. "Please, I think we should go now."

A small hole in the middle surrounded by druid symbols drew her gaze. She kicked off her slippers and stepped on to the table for a closer look.

As she approached the centre, her ears roared and she felt dizzy. Mist curled around the chairs. Seated in some of them were pale, ghostly knights, who stared at the sword in her hand with eager eyes.

She caught her breath, looking vainly for her father's ghost among them. "Who are you?" she whispered. "Can you see me?"

The knights simply watched the sword, which made her feel silly because she had no idea what to do with it next.

"Merlin!" she called, her voice echoing around the hall. "Can you hear me? I've got Excalibur and your pathfinder and we're at Camelot like you said, but we need to know how to get back to Avalon. How do we work the magic to take us through the mists?"

No answer. She looked more carefully at the knights' faces, but didn't recognise any of them. She tried to count them, but kept forgetting where she had started, just as she had with the chairs. They obviously couldn't hear her, and neither could Merlin, wherever he was – there must be something else she needed to do.

She examined the strange hole. It looked about the width of a sword blade. She thought of the songs that told how her father had drawn the sword from the stone. Could it be that simple? With a shiver of excitement, she lifted Excalibur with both hands and lowered the shining tip into the table. It fitted perfectly. Power rushed up her arms, the jewel brightened, and she felt the Round Table tug at the blade. Refusing to let go, she was dragged to her knees.

The ghostly knights leaned forward eagerly, their pale eyes gleaming.

"*Careful…*" they whispered.

A dark-haired lad lounging in the chair

nearest the doors fixed startling green eyes on her and smiled.

"Looking for someone?" he said.

His voice sent a chill through her. He wore no armour, but she'd seen those eyes before: standing behind the bloodbeard in the Saxon camp as he tortured Sir Bors; on the battlefield when the bloodbeard had dragged her off her horse; and in Merlin's song-pictures as his axe came down on her father's head.

"*Mordred!*" Rage filled her. She struggled to pull Excalibur back out of the table. But an invisible force seemed to hold it in place.

The boy leaned back in his chair and put both his hands behind his head. Rhianna stared at them uneasily. Had the dark knight found a way to heal himself? With his smooth chin and long eyelashes, he looked almost as handsome as an Avalonian. "So, cousin," he said. "It seems the tales I've been hearing about you are true. You're braver than I thought you'd be. You might have stolen my Saxon allies with your sweet damsel's tongue, but I have other allies now. Stronger ones than yours, I think."

He smirked at her, then suddenly leaned forward and stared into her eyes. "What's the matter, cousin? Having trouble controlling your sword? Why not give up your silly quest and let me have it? All men have to die in the end, even King Arthur. I expect Merlin told you some nonsense about him coming back to life if you take the Sword of Light back to Avalon? It's not going to happen, any fool can see that. Wounds like the one I gave him do not heal easily. Believe me, it'll be many thousands of years before your father's soul returns to his body, if ever. He's not coming back in either of our lifetimes. Give me the Sword of Light, and maybe I'll let you enjoy the rest of yours as a damsel should, picking flowers and dancing and such, while I look after Excalibur for you."

Rhianna blinked, her thoughts clearing. "Never!" she said. "You're not really here, are you? This is just spirit magic. Your real body doesn't have two hands any more because Merlin told us my father cut one of them off in the battle. You can't hurt me."

"I wouldn't be so sure of that," the boy said. "Remember in the Saxon camp?" He lifted his right hand and closed it very slowly.

Her wrist, where his gauntleted fist had touched her back then, turned cold again. Ice shivered up her arm, and a shadow crossed the stars. She gritted her teeth and held on to Excalibur as tightly as she could.

Of course, he must be lying about her father sleeping in the crystal caverns for thousands of years... but what if he was right? What if she took the sword back to Avalon and King Arthur's body never healed to carry it again? Then Mordred would have plenty of time to get hold of the other three Lights. Despite what Merlin had said back in Lord Avallach's hall about the Lance being broken and the Grail vanishing, three to one didn't sound very good odds. She thought uneasily of her dream, and her arms trembled with sudden doubt.

Mordred smiled. "Give in, cousin. Why struggle so? Merlin's finished. He can't help you now. If you don't trust me with Excalibur, then why not use it yourself? Stop being so feeble. Blood that blade of yours. Until you do, your father's knights will never stop treating you like a child, and the squires will tease you for being a damsel who wants to fight. You'll be just as powerless here in the world of men as you were back in Avalon. Go on, cousin, I know you want to. Pendragon blood runs in your veins, even as it does in mine. Fighting blood. Ambitious blood. It burns you, doesn't it?"

Rhianna gave a final heave, and the blade scraped free in a shower of blue sparks. She leaped across the table and put the sword to Mordred's throat. "Where's Merlin? What did your mother do to him? Is he dead? Tell me!"

The shadow-boy laughed. "Dead enough. The time of the druids is over. Merlin was the last of them, you know. Only his Avalonian blood kept him alive so long; weak fairy blood like your interfering little friend's. Maybe

I should ask Mother to drown your precious fairy prince, too? Can't swim, can he? Afraid of water, like all Avalonians. You'd give me the Sword of Light then, maybe—"

Rhianna's ears roared. Excalibur's jewel darkened, and the sword took on a life of its own, just as it had when she'd been fighting the bloodbeard on the battlefield. She grasped the hilt two-handed and swung the blade at her cousin's mocking smile—

"NO, RHIA!"

As Elphin's harp tinkled across the vast hall, Mordred's shadow vanished. The jewel brightened again, revealing Arianrhod cowering behind the empty chair with her hands over her head. Rhianna came to her senses with a shudder. She'd almost cut the poor girl's throat!

She lowered the blade with trembling arms, and the pale knights faded, leaving her standing barefoot on the Round Table in her nightgown holding Excalibur. A crowd of squires, also in their nightclothes, were staring at her. Some carried torches, others daggers. She saw Gareth near the front, smirking at her, and flushed.

Arianrhod hurried back around the table to bring her the cloak she'd left on a chair. Rhianna put it on. With as much dignity as she could manage, she sheathed Excalibur and jumped lightly to the floor.

"Well, what are you all staring at?" she said, rubbing her numb wrist. "You're not supposed to be in here, are you?"

"You're not supposed to be in here, either, Damsel Rhianna," Cai pointed out, pushing to the front of the crowd. "I told you that table's magic. It can be dangerous if you don't know what you're doing. Lucky Elphin here woke up and heard you."

Rhianna glanced at her friend. His fingers were freshly bandaged – he had been plucking his harp with his thumbs. She looked up at the hole in the roof. The stars were paling. She shivered.

"Lucky for you, most of the knights are still sleepin' off their mead," Cai said. "Or you'd be in a *lot* of trouble." He peered closer at Arianrhod and scowled. "Hey, ain't you Morgan Le Fay's maid? Keep away from Damsel Rhianna, you little witch!"

Arianrhod ducked his waving dagger and raised her hands to protect her face – with good reason, since Cai's weaponry skills were no better than his riding.

"Stop it, Cai!" Rhianna snapped, still feeling shaky after her encounter with Mordred's shadow. "I asked her to bring me here. She's not working for Mordred's mother any more, you dolt. Can't you see what Lady Morgan did to her face?"

Elphin gave Arianrhod's cheek a closer look and frowned. He plucked another chord. "Better?" he said. "I can't make the scars go away, but that should help with the pain."

Arianrhod smiled shyly at the Avalonian prince and touched her cheek in wonder. "Much better," she said. "Thank you."

Cai made a face. "If you two have quite finished, we'd better get out of here before someone comes…"

"Too late," Gareth said with another smirk.

The commotion in the Great Hall had

attracted the attention of the sentries, who had raised the alarm. Sir Agravaine ducked through the little door and snapped out orders. A bar scraped back, and one of the huge doors creaked open to admit a furious Sir Bors.

"Out, the lot of you!" he bellowed. "Now!"

The squires, who had gathered around Rhianna for a closer look at Excalibur, filed out of the hall casting her backwards glances.

"Is she really King Arthur's daughter?"

"Don't look much like a princess to me."

"Never mind the girls," someone else said. "Did anyone spot that dirty sneak Mordred? I'm sure I saw him in here! Where'd he go? He needs teachin' a lesson, the traitor…"

Finally, the boys were gone, leaving the hall humming with the echoes of magic. Rhianna faced the angry knights and tried to look like a princess. Not easy in her nightdress with her bare feet and hacked hair.

Sir Bors scowled at her. "Since I woke up yesterday morning, I've fought in a battle, sorted out the mess that idiot Lancelot left behind, fed an army, bandaged up my wounded men, seen to the horses, and got to bed about a heartbeat ago," he said. "I got a headache – and the last thing I want is to hear your fairy harp in here!" He turned his scowl on Elphin, who quickly silenced the strings and stared at the circle of sky.

"Would one of you care to explain exactly what Damsel Rhianna was doing dancing on the Round Table in the middle of the night?" Sir Agravaine said.

"Weren't my idea," Cai said quickly. "I was asleep. Ask the witch's maid!"

"I don't think it was Rhianna's fault," Elphin said, stroking the stone with a bandaged hand. "This table has almost as much power as my father's palace back in Avalon. I expect it called to the sword."

"I'm sorry…" Arianrhod began.

Rhianna waved them all silent. "It was my idea. I wanted to see if I could contact Merlin. When I was standing on it, I saw some knights sitting around the table." She decided not to mention her cousin Mordred. "Who were they?"

Sir Bors sank into one of the big chairs. He put a cushion behind his head and closed his eyes. "They're the knights who died on the Grail Quest, Damsel Rhianna. We see them in here sometimes. They're just ghosts. Don't worry about them. At least you didn't get as far as sheathing Excalibur in the Round Table to call a living soul. There's some of them as used to sit in here we don't want snooping around Camelot these days."

Rhianna swallowed. No wonder Mordred's shadow had been able to reach her so easily. She'd as good as invited him in!

"Is that how my father used to contact Merlin when he was away?" she asked innocently.

"Yes." Sir Bors said with a sigh. "With Excalibur, Arthur could contact anybody who has ever sat in here, living or dead. But before you try the magic, we need to be here to help you. All of us, without headaches, and in the daylight so we can see who we're talking to. So do you think you can possibly wait a few days more, Damsel Rhianna?"

Elphin nodded, agreeing with Sir Bors.

"And my fingers need to heal properly so I can play my harp if you need me to." Again his gaze met hers, and she knew he meant if Mordred appeared again.

"And you should be dressed like a princess," added Arianrhod. "So if King Arthur sees you from Avalon, he'll know who you are."

"Yeah, and to show Gareth and them other cheeky squires not to mess with you, Damsel Rhianna!" Cai added.

Rhianna sighed. She needed to contact Merlin more than ever, after what Mordred had said. But at least she knew how the magic worked now. "Then I suppose I'd better wait," she said.

◀◙ 12 ◙▶

Snowed In

That year the snow fell thick and deep
And Mordred's power at last did sleep;
While in body small and feathered
Merlin's druid soul was tethered.

The blizzard continued for days. Snow covered the pit where the dead had been buried, laid white fur along the branches of the trees, and filled the ditches where men had spilled their blood. It made the world seem clean again.

Rhianna woke late after her encounter with Mordred, feeling grumpy and sore. She was tempted to stay in bed until the knights arranged their meeting of the Round Table. But Arianrhod seemed determined to use the time to turn her into a princess, and led her to the royal bathroom. Rhianna frowned at the pool of steaming water in the middle of the chamber. "But what's it for?" she said, confused.

The girl giggled. "To wash yourself in, of course. The queen loved to bathe in here. It's a Roman thing, really, but it's good fun." She eyed Rhianna sideways. "Your father used it after he'd had a hard fight. Why not try it, and I'll bring your breakfast while you bathe?"

At the promise of breakfast, Rhianna gave in. Soon she was soaking in the warm water, munching honey cakes, while Arianrhod washed her hair yet again and offered her scented oils to scrub the dirt from her skin. Her aches and pains vanished... the bath worked almost as well as Elphin's harp. She looked for her father's ghost in the steam, but it did not appear. Strange to think this huge stone fortress could have been her home. Her parents had walked along these corridors, eaten in the huge dining hall and slept in one of the great beds.

Lady Isabel came to inspect the result. She smiled as she fixed a narrow gold band in Rhianna's hair. "Much better," she said. "Now, I know you're not used to our ways yet, Rhianna, but in Camelot damsels don't run around the corridors in their nightclothes brandishing swords. I'd lock Excalibur in the armoury, if it weren't your father's magic sword. Sir Bors thinks it'll be safer in the tower with you, but you've got to promise not to frighten the other girls with it. I've put a chest in your room where you can keep it with your armour and your other things." She gave Rhianna a bemused look then smiled again. "Well, I suppose it'll make a change to have a female Pendragon! Everyone's talking about the treaty you made with the Saxon chief. That's the most sensible thing anyone around here's done for some time. Maybe we won't get so many wounded knights limping home from the wars to bandage up in future."

Rhianna felt unexpectedly shy before the tall, golden-haired woman who had kissed her as she slept. "I hope not, Lady Isabel," she said, remembering her father's terrible wounds. What if Mordred was right about them never healing?

Later, when she showed him the bathroom,

Elphin took one look at the pool and his eyes whirled violet. "You're not getting me in there!" he said, shuddering a little.

Rhianna smiled. "How do the squires get clean, then?"

"There's buckets and sponges for when they can't get down to the river. That'll do me until I can play my harp again."

She eyed his bandaged fingers. "How long?"

"Not long – a few days, maybe." His eyes darkened. "I won't let Mordred's magic reach you again, Rhia, don't worry."

"I'm not worried about Mordred," she said, though the dark knight had scared her more than she liked to admit. "But I've got to speak to Merlin as soon as possible. He told me to look for the dragon... I thought he meant the shadrake, since it brought me his pathfinder, but maybe he meant a statue or something? We might as well look everywhere while we're waiting."

She'd already noticed the creatures were all over the place – carved into the backs of chairs, embroidered across the Pendragon's banners and wall hangings, and snarling down at them from the battlements.

"Are you sure you're feeling strong enough, my lady?" Arianrhod said. "Camelot's a big castle."

"Then we'd better start now!" she leaned into the pool and splashed her friends with water to get them moving.

All outside training had been cancelled due to the weather, so Cai got let off lessons to join them. First they visited the stables with their dragonhead posts, where Rhianna was relieved to see Alba happily munching hay in a big stall between Sir Bors' bay stallion and Elphin's little Evenstar.

The mare whinnied a joyful welcome and searched her with a soft muzzle. *Where are my apples?*

"Oh, beautiful one!" Rhianna laughed. "I forgot. I'll find you some."

But the apple store had been raided for the feast. All she could offer the mist horse was a bruised core Cai reluctantly produced from his pocket. Alba ate the mushy offering with great dignity, while Rhianna straightened her mane and wondered how long it would be before they saw Avalon again.

"I asked Camelot's smith to put Evenstar's shoes back on," Elphin told her quietly. "He had to use different nails because the Saxons lost the ones Father's smith used. I just hope the magic still works."

"You can check with Merlin when he turns up," Rhianna said. When her friend went quiet, she punched him on the arm. "Cheer up, if this weather carries on much longer all the water will be frozen anyway and we'll be able to ride across the ice."

"You're on your own if you do," Cai said, giving them a sideways look. "This clumsy beast'd crack it with his first step." But he patted the bay horse and promised to exercise him as soon as they could get out.

Rhianna kissed Alba's nose and promised to bring her more apples soon. "What's through there?"

Cai took them next door to the mews, where rows of fluffed-out birds wearing little hoods dozed on their perches. Some were large and fierce looking, others quite small.

The whole building smelled musty.

Rhianna sneezed, making a small blue-grey bird in the shadows at the back flutter its tattered wings. It had freckles on its breast like the ones on her nose, and something about it made her look closer. "That's one of the birds that attacked the shadrake!" she said, remembering how it had been tumbled through the air by the dragon and glad to see it had survived the battle.

Cai frowned. "It's a merlin. Must be a new one. Hope I don't get the job of training it. They don't look very big, but they've got sharp claws."

While the boy grumbled on about how many times he had been scratched by hawks, Rhianna eyed the dusty sunbeams full of drifting feathers and smiled at the thought of her father's druid being named after a tiny bird. "Where to next?" she said.

Cai took them to the armoury, where the knights' jousting lances were stacked neatly around the walls with their shields and armour, and then the kitchens, where he stole four warm pies from a tray and got told off by the cook. "Those are for the midwinter feast, young squire!" she called after them, as they ran out of the door giggling.

Cai seemed content to hang around the kitchen door. But Rhianna wasn't hungry. She finished her pie and frowned at the falling snow.

Even the weather seemed determined to stop her taking the Sword of Light back to Avalon. She realised the only people they'd seen on her tour of the castle were servants and women. She felt suddenly suspicious. What if the knights didn't want her quest to succeed?

What if they had really meant to keep Excalibur at Camelot, all along? Could that be why they were taking so long to organise a meeting of the Round Table?

"Where's Sir Bors?" she asked Cai as they dashed back through the blizzard to the main building. "And what about the rest of the knights? Why aren't they polishing their shields, or whatever they usually do indoors when it snows?"

"Er…" Cai blushed and looked towards the Great Hall.

Then she knew. "They've called a meeting of the Round Table, haven't they? Without me!"

Arianrhod gave her a stricken look. "Those meetings always go on for ages, and Lady Isabel said you needed your rest.

"Sir Bors promised he'd tell you when

they're ready to try the magic," Cai said. "Next month, maybe."

"Next *month*?" Rhianna stared at her friends in disbelief. "Mordred might have raised another army by then!"

"I haven't finished hemming your new dress…" Arianrhod protested.

"And my fingers are still rather sore, Rhia," Elphin said. "It might be better to wait until the snow stops and—"

"And what?" Rhianna turned so suddenly to face her friend, he had to use a quick flick of his hand to mist the air between them and avoid walking straight into her. She looked accusingly at his hand. "Fingers still sore, are they?" she said. "Let me see! Arianrhod, help me with his bandages."

Elphin sighed and allowed them to unwind

the linen. His slender Avalonian fingers showed pale scars, but no blisters. Rhianna blinked at them in confusion.

Her friend met her accusing gaze with whirling purple eyes. "We just think you should wait a bit longer before you try using Excalibur in the Round Table again. After all, Merlin didn't tell you to meet him there. Maybe he knew it was too dangerous. What if something goes wrong again?"

She knew what he meant: if Mordred tried to reach her with his dark magic.

"It won't," she said firmly. "I'll be ready for Mordred's tricks next time. Besides, it's only some kind of spirit magic, isn't it? Words can't hurt me."

Elphin frowned. "Words can be just as dangerous as weapons – you nearly killed poor

Arianrhod last night! It'd be safer to wait. The Wild Hunt rides into the world of men at midwinter remember? That's only a few days away now. Father might know what happened to Merlin. Maybe we can ride back to Avalon with them, or at least give Excalibur to Father so he can take it back through the mists where it'll be safe."

Rhianna stared at her friend. The Wild Hunt – how could she have forgotten? "I'm sure Merlin wouldn't have told me to bring Excalibur to Camelot if the Wild Hunt could take it back to Avalon," she said uneasily.

"Rhia, we've no proof that message came from Merlin. What if it was meant to lure us into a trap?"

True, when they reached Camelot they'd ridden straight into the Saxon army…

and when she'd tried the magic in the Round Table Mordred had almost tricked her into blooding Excalibur. She shook her head. "It must have come from Merlin! He sent us his pathfinder like he said he would, didn't he?"

"Or maybe *Morgan Le Fay* sent it, with that shadrake." Elphin's eyes whirled violet. "We can't risk using it until we know it's not a trap. Father will help us, I'm sure he will."

"All right…" she said, still not happy. "If we don't manage to contact Merlin before midwinter, then we can look for the Hunt. But I'm not taking Excalibur back to Avalon until I'm sure my father will wake up to carry it. Agreed?"

"That sword's changed you," her friend said sadly. "Father warned me this might happen. I think you want King Arthur to sleep in the crystal caverns for ever so you can be some kind of heroine, battling dragons and fighting Saxons in his place."

"That's not true!"

"Isn't it? After all, you never really knew him. Why should you care if he's reborn or not?"

"Because he's my *father* and Mordred *killed him!*" Rhianna's eyes pricked with angry tears. "You wouldn't understand. Your father will never die. Besides, I do know him... sort of, anyway. I've seen his ghost several times now, and I've heard it speak to me, too. He knows who I am now. He helped me fight Mordred's shadow during the battle, and he spoke to Sir Bors before we went to the lake. I told you that, remember?"

Elphin sighed. "You were asleep, Rhia, and so was Sir Bors. You were asleep when you got Merlin's message, too. Father says humans dream things sometimes, if they want them badly enough."

"I'm not imagining things." Rhianna glared at him. "I wasn't asleep during the battle, was I? Ask Arianrhod – she saw him too."

"You told me it was magic, Rhia," the girl whispered.

"I thought the whole reason we came here was to find Excalibur and take it back to Avalon to keep it out of Mordred's hands?" Elphin said more gently.

Rhianna gritted her teeth. "That might be why you came! I came because I thought my father would be reborn to carry it and finish his battle against Mordred. Only now I'm not sure he'll return in time to stop Mordred from getting hold of the other three Lights, if he wakes up at all…" She choked. But Mordred had to be lying. "The Sword of Light protects Camelot, doesn't it? We can't take Excalibur back to Avalon and leave everyone here in danger. We have to find out how long it'll be before King Arthur heals first. Anyway, I want to see my mother before I go back – surely you can understand that?"

Arianrhod fingered her scar and coughed nervously.

"Do you want me to tell Sir Bors you're ready to join the meeting, or not?" Cai said.

Rhianna eyed Elphin again. "If you're scared, I'll understand. You don't have to come. I'll be fine with the knights to protect me."

Her friend shook his dark curls. "I'll be there," he said in a resigned tone. "Just give me time to tune my harp."

Rhianna's neck prickled as she entered the Great Hall with Excalibur. But this time it was daylight, and torches in the alcoves banished the final shadows. Snowflakes drifted through the hole in the roof and melted on the blue stone, making the druid marks gleam. Arianrhod had done her best at short notice with the dress, tacking up the hem so it wouldn't trip her. It was of thick green wool, heavy but warm. A golden circlet tamed her sweet-smelling hair, and she wore her embroidered slippers. Elphin followed with his harp, unusually quiet.

The hall was full of knights, some seated around the table, others standing in muttering groups. Sir Bors was there, of course, with Sir Bedivere on his left and Sir Agravaine next to him. Mordred's seat remained empty.

She recognised some of the fighters from the camp, but many were the old men who had stayed to defend Camelot. They had brought along their shields, which hung on the backs of their chairs. Rhianna was the only one with a sword.

The two sentries standing guard outside slammed the doors shut behind her with a clang that echoed through her bones. Some of the knights looked curiously at her as Sir Bors beckoned her over. The rest carried on talking among themselves.

Rhianna opened her mouth to ask why they had started without her. But Sir Bors pushed her into the seat next to him and slammed his hand down on the table. "Right, let's get on with it!" he said. "We've brought Arthur's daughter out of Avalon and we've made peace with the Saxons for now. But there'll be more barbarians to deal with in the spring, so we need to make plans for next year's campaign. Also, the people will expect their midwinter feast and a joust to kick off the season. We need to carry on as normal to show we are back in control of Camelot."

At this, shouts of ridicule broke out.

"Feast? We've been fightin' all harvest time! We've hardly enough rations to last the winter, as it is."

"Yeah, and who's going to lead this great spring campaign? The damsel here on her white pony? She's brave enough, I'll give her that. But it's one thing to see off a half-beaten Saxon rabble on our home ground, and quite another to meet a barbarian army in the field."

"And what about Prince Mordred? He could

be busy raising another army, for all we know. Arthur's dead, so we got to face facts. First thing we should do is elect a new war leader."

This caused a lot more shouting and arguments as to who should take over from Arthur. Some favoured Sir Bors, who had proved himself by bringing Rhianna safely to Camelot. Others mentioned Sir Bedivere, to whom Arthur had first entrusted Excalibur – but were laughed down at the thought of 'Soft Hands' leading them in battle. Quite a few wanted to go after Sir Lancelot and teach him a lesson.

A grizzled old knight looked at Rhianna in a way that made her skin crawl. "At least we've got Excalibur," he said. "We can always sit the girl on the throne for now to keep the people happy until we find a suitable husband for her."

Rhianna stared at him in horror. "No you can't!" she protested, but nobody took any notice.

She frowned as their voices grew louder and their big, scarred fists thumped the stone. She began to see why her father had forbidden his knights to carry weapons in here. Avalonians never yelled at each other like this. They listened when people sang, and then sang in their own turn. The knights were talking over her head as if she were some kind of trophy, a thing with no feelings of her own. Had they forgotten already how she'd rescued Excalibur from the Lady of the Lake, fought the shadrake and made a peace treaty with the Saxon chief Cynric?

She kicked off her slippers, stood on her chair and drew Excalibur in a hiss of silver sparks.

"Careful, Rhia..." Elphin warned.

"Just get your harp ready," she told him as she stepped onto the Round Table.

The men were all arguing so loudly, she had reached the centre before anyone noticed. Snowflakes drifted through the hole in the roof and melted in her hair. Her hands felt sweaty and cold at the same time. She held Excalibur over the opening and took a deep breath.

Behind her, she heard Elphin begin to strum lightly on his harp.

"Shut up, all of you!" she yelled with her powerful lungs. The knights stopped arguing mid-sentence as Excalibur's white jewel brightened in response to her voice. They stared warily at the sword. Some of the men paled as they realised what she was about to do.

"We're not here to discuss electing a new

war leader," Rhianna continued. "My father will return soon to lead you himself. All I have to do is get Excalibur back to Avalon for him."

There was an uneasy silence.

"That dragon must've sent the girl crazy," an older knight grumbled. "Arthur's not comin' back from the dead, magic sword or no magic sword."

"Let's ask Merlin that, shall we?" Rhianna said. Before anybody else could speak, she plunged the Sword of Light into the Round Table.

She braced herself for the powerful tug she'd felt on the first night, but this time it felt more like forcing the blade into mud. Elphin played heroically, filling the vast hall with enchantments. The air sparkled. Rhianna glanced warily around the table, but to her relief there was no sign of

Mordred's shadow. No ghostly knights this time, either. She eyed the chair she'd just vacated, hoping for a glimpse of her father's ghost, but the Pendragon's seat remained empty. Behind it, Elphin's fingers moved faster across the strings of his harp. She saw beads of sweat on her friend's forehead and knew he wouldn't be able to keep up the magic for much longer.

"Merlin!" she called. "Can you hear me? It's Rhianna! I'm at the Round Table. I've got your pathfinder and Excalibur, and all the knights are here. They want to know when King Arthur will return to lead them." *Please don't say thousands of years*, she willed.

She gripped the hilt until her arms trembled with effort. But no answer came.

She sighed in disappointment and let Excalibur spring from the stone. Reluctantly, she sheathed the glimmering blade and returned to her seat.

The knights sighed, too. "Never mind, Damsel Rhianna," Sir Bedivere said, giving her a sympathetic pat on the arm. "It was worth a try. Obviously only Arthur himself can work the magic that lets us speak to souls." He sounded a bit relieved, and there were nods and mutters of agreement around the table.

Elphin let his harp fall silent. He sat on the floor behind her chair, cradling his harp, his head bowed in weariness. She felt a pang of guilt. Had she made him play too soon? By now the knights were all looking at her, whispering restlessly. One or two muttered that damsels should stick to their embroidery and leave the business of running the kingdom to men.

Rhianna's blood rose. She'd just have to do

this without magic, the way she always used to. Before the knights could start arguing again, she lifted her chin and said, "Cai told us everyone who sits at King Arthur's Round Table has an equal voice. Is that true?"

Sir Bedivere smiled. "That's right. Princess Rhianna has a voice, too. Let's hear what she has to say."

Rhianna ignored the sniggerers who said she certainly had a loud voice for a damsel. She laid Excalibur on the table in front of her, rested her hands on the white jewel and lifted her chin. "I'm too young to get married, and Camelot already has a queen. I think you should send word to Sir Lancelot and tell him to bring my mother back as soon as the snow stops. He was King Arthur's champion knight, wasn't he? He can lead you until my father gets back from Avalon."

"Ha!" muttered the grizzled knight who had wanted to marry her off. "I can just see Lancelot agreeing to that."

But another knight said, "The girl's got a point. Let Lancelot make up for what he did by leading us against the barbarians. I'd like to see his face when King Arthur rides back from the dead to reclaim Guinevere."

This roused a few chuckles. She even saw Sir Agravaine's lips twitch in amusement. Sir Bedivere smiled at her again in approval, and some of the older knights nodded.

"Right!" Sir Bors said. "You heard the princess! We'll send some men north to fetch Lancelot back as soon as the weather clears. I'm sure the queen will persuade him to return once she knows Princess Rhianna is here. In the meantime, we'll organise the best feast we can and start making plans for the spring joust. Hopefully, Cynric's promise will hold for a bit – we'd best send a scribe after him to get it written up, proper like. Rhianna's right. There'll be quite enough fightin' to keep us occupied next year, without us killing each other over the winter."

"And if some of you still want to slog it out with Lancelot, you can always enter the spring joust," Sir Agravaine added with a grin. "I think we might even let young Cai enter the squires' tilt this year, since he seems to have learned how to sit a horse at last."

This caused a rumble of laughter among the knights, and when they began their discussion again it was with much better humour. Rhianna turned in her chair and gave Elphin a suspicious look. Her friend, who looked a bit happier now, lifted his harp and winked.

After their failure to contact Merlin, Rhianna was worried the blizzard might continue so they couldn't look for the Hunt. She kept thinking of how Elphin had told her they hunted lost souls, and of her father's ghost still out there somewhere in the snow. What if the Hunt took King Arthur's soul to Annwn by mistake? She got her boots and thickest cloak ready in case they had to go out in the storm.

But on midwinter's day, as if by magic, the weather finally cleared. The squires and damsels started a snowball fight in the courtyard, shrieking and laughing in the bright winter sunshine. Even Arianrhod smiled as a snowball broke in her hair – thrown by Cai, who had actually been aiming at Gareth. The older boy

and his friends seemed to resent Rhianna even
more now that everyone had accepted her as
King Arthur's daughter. And since Elphin no
longer needed his bandages, everyone could see
he wasn't human, which didn't help.

"What's the matter, Cai?" Gareth called.
"Still can't aim straight? Or are you after the
witch's maid? Been hanging around with her a
lot lately, you and that fairy boy."

Arianrhod blushed. Red-faced, Cai knocked
Gareth down. The other boys crowded round
to cheer the fight.

A pair of knights trotted past on snorting,
frisky horses with scrolls sticking out of their
saddlebags. "Don't kill each other yet, lads!"
they called with a chuckle. "Save it for the tilt,
then we can all watch." The outer gates of
Camelot opened for the first time since the

storm, and the men galloped through in a spray of ice and disappeared along the Roman road, leaving two neat trails of prints.

Elphin caught Rhianna's eye and jerked his head at the stables. She nodded, and they slipped away to saddle their mist horses.

◀▮ 13 ▮▶

Wild Hunt

Midwinter the fairy host did ride;
Souls of men to their saddles tied,
When brave Rhianna challenged their lord
To a bloodless duel for the sword.

As they mounted, Rhianna knew they should probably ask for an escort. But the Saxon threat had gone, and the old knights Sir Bors would have sent with them would only have slowed them down. Anyway, she had brought Excalibur, and Elphin had his harp.

Before anyone could stop them, they were through the gates and trotting down the hill.

My legs are stiff, Alba complained, tossing her head. *I want to gallop.*

Rhianna stopped looking for ghosts and grinned. "So do I!" As soon as they reached flatter ground, she let Alba break into a canter. It felt good to be out riding again after being cooped up inside playing the princess for so long. Alba threw several bucks, glad to be out of the castle as well, while Evenstar mischievously misted around the Saxon funeral pyres.

Elphin glanced across at her, a challenge in his eyes. "Race?" Not waiting for an answer, he urged Evenstar into the trees. She sent Alba after him, ducking snow-laden branches, twisting and turning along the narrow paths. She laughed as the snow crystals sprayed her face. It felt good to be out riding with her friend – like the old days back in Avalon, only colder. They pulled up, panting, in a holly glade surrounded by scarlet berries.

"You're getting faster," Rhianna observed.

Elphin smiled. "I have to keep up with you, in case you decide to have another duel with Mordred's shadow while I'm not around."

Rhianna sobered. She brushed some twigs from Excalibur's scabbard and fiddled with Alba's mane, still a bit disappointed her father's ghost had not been waiting for them outside the gates. "So how do we find the Hunt?"

Elphin studied the wood. "We could always ride to the Lonely Tor and wait for them there. If we miss them, I could try using Merlin's pathfinder to take us through the mists."

"Not after what happened to Merlin!"

Rhianna frowned at him. "You said it might be a trap, remember? What if the shadrake comes again? Besides, I left the pathfinder in my room and the Tor's several days' ride away. Sir Bors would have a heart attack if we went missing for that long. I haven't seen my father's ghost since the battle, and Sir Lancelot's ridden off with my mother. If I lose you as well, I don't know what I'll do." The words stuck in her throat.

Elphin patted her arm. His fingers had calluses from the strings of his harp, but his touch remained gentle. "You'd still have Cai," he teased. "He worships the ground you walk on."

She scowled. "Great! A champion who can't aim straight, drops his wooden sword at the first blow and falls off every time his horse goes faster than a trot!"

"That's not fair," Elphin said. "Cai's trying his

best. It takes courage to learn to ride the way he did, chased by enemies and dragons. He looks after me in the squires' dormitory, you know."

Rhianna sighed. "I know. That reminds me… when Sir Lancelot comes back to lead the knights, we should ask him to show us that magic lance Cai told us about, the one he broke. If it's the Lance of Truth, do you think you could use your harp to mend it? Then we'd have two of the Lights, so even if Mordred finds the Crown we should be able to hold Camelot against him."

Elphin watched her with his violet eyes. "It'd be safer to take Excalibur back to Avalon now, if we can."

She knew what he meant. Before she blooded the blade.

"Well, we can't without Merlin's help,

can we?" she said impatiently. "So I might as well use it in the meantime. I'm not intending to fight Mordred myself. The knights will do that." But even as she spoke, she imagined Alba rearing over her cowering cousin while she sliced Excalibur across his arrogant smile.

"Rhia," Elphin said in a gentle voice. "I need to tell you something."

"What?"

"At the meeting in the Great Hall, when I played my harp, I *stopped* the magic. That's why you couldn't contact anyone with Excalibur."

She blinked at him. "You stopped the magic?" Confusion filled her. "But… why?"

"There were a lot of unarmed knights sitting around that table. I couldn't risk Mordred's magic influencing you again. But don't worry, because I'm sure Father will know what to do."

He reached for his harp. "Keep quiet a moment. I think this will work." He ran his fingers across the strings and a wild trill rippled out into the wood.

She felt dizzy. She had never heard him play such music before, and it made her hair stand on end. She scowled at her friend, unable to believe he had tricked her. Did he really think she wasn't strong enough to control her sword? She opened her mouth to tell him not to be so silly, and that the Hunt could be anywhere – it would never hear him. Then something came rushing through the trees towards them. Alba misted under her, but she somehow stayed in the saddle.

You did not fall off me, the mare said, pleased.

There was no time to think about this. A third horse had joined them, pale and luminous as their own mounts. It pawed the snow and snorted. Its rider wore a circlet of gold around his wild black hair. His cloak of midnight blue brushed the ground, glittering with mist magic. His purple gaze fixed on Excalibur, and the jewel warmed under Rhianna's palm in response.

"*Faha'ruh*," said the newcomer, raising his six-fingered hand.

"Father!" Elphin said, his face lighting up with relief and joy. "You came!"

"Lord Avallach," Rhianna said warily. She started to wonder if the Avalonian lord and his son had planned from the start to bring her here alone with the Sword of Light. She gripped Alba's reins, ready to turn and gallop if she needed to. "Is Merlin with you? We lost him in the mists. He said he'd meet us at Camelot, but he hasn't turned up yet."

The Avalonian lord regarded her kindly. "I'm sorry to say we found Merlin's body under the water on our way out of Avalon. His druid spirit was gone from it."

Rhianna clenched her fists. So Mordred had been telling the truth about that, at least. "Do you know where it went?"

"No, my child, I'm afraid not. Druids have their own ways of escaping death. But we heard your call. We've been hunting the souls released from their bodies by the battle. They gave us a good chase. After we've taken them into the mists, we'll be heading back to Avalon. If you wish you can ride with us. But we have to go now. The Hunt must return before nightfall."

Rhianna became aware of more luminous horses in the woods around them. Their riders rustled through the branches, ghostly and transparent, reminding her of the pale knights in the Great Hall of Camelot. Some were human – ancient heroes reborn to ride again. Tied over the mist horses' saddles, thin twists of darkness writhed and screamed with faint men's voices. She looked anxiously for her father's ghost, but to her relief he was not among them.

She shivered. "You mean… take our souls?" she whispered.

"Don't be silly," Elphin said. But he eyed his father a bit uncertainly.

"I mean, Rhianna Pendragon, that it's time for you to choose. You can ride Alba back to Avalon with us now. Or you can choose to stay in the world of men with your own people. But be warned. If you stay, you might never see your father again."

Another shiver went through her. "But surely my father will return to Camelot when he's reborn?" She rested her hand on Excalibur's white jewel. Just let him try lying to her.

The Avalonian lord tightened his lips. "The mists are thickening. The dark powers of Annwn grow stronger by the day. Even the Hunt found the way difficult this year. No, my child. Arthur will remain with us for many years yet."

As Rhianna tried to think, they heard twigs snapping in the trees behind them and shrill voices in the distance. She thought she heard Cai calling her name. The Avalonian host rippled uneasily, and the bound souls twisted and screamed.

"Hurry!" said Lord Avallach. "Make your choice, or we might have to take your friends' souls with us when we leave."

Rhianna sat very straight in her saddle. She thought briefly of being back in Avalon, safe from her cousin Mordred and the dark magic of Annwn. Then she thought of the mother she had not yet met, of Arianrhod and Cai and all the people back at Camelot relying on the Sword of Light to protect them, and of her father's voice saying *"Courage, daughter"*. Even if she had been imagining his ghost, she couldn't abandon her new friends to Mordred's bloodbeards.

"I'm staying!" she said. "I'm not afraid."

"I'm staying with Rhianna," Elphin said quickly, his fingers tightening on his reins.

She gave him a surprised glance.

Lord Avallach frowned at his son. "Are you sure? The world of men has already scarred your hands. It may scar you many more times before you are finished here."

"I know that, Father," Elphin said. "But humans get hurt all the time and they just put up with it. I have my magic. It's not so bad."

Lord Avallach sighed and turned his purple gaze on Rhianna. "I can understand why you should want to stay among your own people, and it's clear you've enchanted my son with your human spirit. If he wants to watch you grow old, then that's up to him. But give me the Sword of Light so I can return it safely to Avalon." He held out his hand.

"No," Rhianna said, keeping her own hand on the white jewel. Her heart beat faster. "I need it."

"Better do what he says, Rhia!" Elphin hissed as his father's gaze darkened. "Quickly!"

"If Mordred gets hold of all four Lights our magic will fail, and King Arthur will never be reborn," Lord Avallach warned.

"So everyone keeps telling me! I *know*."

"Then give Excalibur to me, my child, and I will keep the Sword of Light safe from Mordred until Arthur wakes to carry it again."

"Which will not be in my lifetime, will it?" she said, her eyes filling with tears. "That's what none of you dared tell me! You let me think I'd live to see my father reborn. I want to know the truth! Will King Arthur return to Camelot if I give you Excalibur?"

"No," Lord Avallach said with a sigh. "Arthur's body is not healing as well as it should, and his spirit still roams the mortal world. It's no good the Hunt taking it back by force, even if we could catch it. An unwilling soul cannot be reunited with its body. Things have gone very wrong here in the world of men. Your father made mistakes. Mordred's poisoned what could have been the greatest kingdom on earth. The balance of power must be restored, and the surviving Lights kept out of the dark knight's hands. Then, maybe, another king will be born strong enough to heal the land. But it's unlikely to be Arthur. He lost his chance when Mordred's blood stained Excalibur."

"But Lady Nimue said she'd cleansed the blade," Rhianna said.

Lord Avallach rode his horse closer and touched the glowing hilt. "The blade, yes. But Excalibur's true magic lies in this jewel, which can call on the spirits of everyone the Pendragon knighted with it, living or dead. Arthur used it well. I sense the strength of many brave men in here, but I also sense a darker presence... your cousin Mordred's. I can't remove the dark spirit without destroying the others – they are too tangled together. Only unforging the sword will cleanse it completely of Mordred's influence, and that can be done nowhere but in Avalon. I'm sorry, child."

Rhianna's head spun. So that was what Nimue had meant when she'd said she couldn't cleanse the hilt? Spirit magic. The strength of a hundred men… Sir Bors, Sir Bedivere, Sir Agravaine, all those dead knights… and Mordred. The very thought made her want to cast the sword from her in disgust. But she kept her hand firm on the white jewel.

"I'll find a way to control it," she said through gritted teeth. "We'll mend the Lance of Truth and find the Crown of Dreams. The Grail of Stars as well, if we need to! That'll heal King Arthur and get rid of Mordred, won't it?"

"The Grail," whispered the Avalonian host.

A hush fell over the clearing. Even the screaming souls quietened. Lord Avallach stared at her with fierce interest, much as Merlin had done at the start of their quest back in Avalon. "It's true the old songs say whoever holds all four Lights can command death itself," he said. "But what makes you think a damsel can succeed where so many of Arthur's best knights failed?"

"This!" Rhianna said, drawing Excalibur in a shining hiss of sparks. The Avalonians sucked in their breath as she showed their lord the gleaming silver blade. "I carried the Sword of Light in battle, fought a dragon, made peace with the Saxons and kept it clean. Look! That's more than my father managed to do, isn't it?"

Lord Avallach did not flinch. "You've been strong enough to resist Mordred's influence so far. But if you keep this sword, the forces of Annwn will never cease from tempting you into using it for evil. See how sharp Excalibur is? See how easy it would be to fail your quest…?" He ran his thumbnail along the edge, shaving off a pale curl, and suddenly closed his hand on the shining blade. "Let me take the temptation from you, child."

His grip was strong and commanding. His eyes flashed, daring her to defy him. The air glittered with ice crystals, making Rhianna dizzy.

Elphin sat frozen in his saddle, his gaze on the glimmering blade caught between his father's hand and hers. Alba pawed at the snow, impatient. The Avalonians watched the strange duel with all their attention. Rhianna saw movement out of the corner of her eye, but held the sword steady so it would not cut Lord Avallach.

"I won't fail," she said. But her heart pounded. Where was her father's ghost when she needed it?

When a big bay horse burst through the undergrowth with two small figures bouncing on its bare back, no one moved to stop it.

"Keep away from Damsel Rhianna, you!" Cai yelled, brandishing his dagger.

With blood-curdling yells, the squires and damsels from the snowball fight in the courtyard raced into the clearing and surrounded Lord Avallach. Some had balls of ice in their fists, which they threw at the Hunt as they passed. These missiles passed right through the ghostly riders, but they scraped up more snow and stood their ground.

The Avalonian lord, clearly startled, opened his fingers and released Excalibur. Rhianna quickly sheathed the blade and let go of the hilt. She discovered she was sweating. She wiped her hands on Alba's mane. No wonder Mordred's shadow had been able to reach her so easily. His spirit had been lurking in Excalibur's hilt all this time! She thought she understood a bit better how the dark knight had been able to kill a great hero like her father.

Arianrhod – the second rider – let go of Cai's waist, slithered to the ground and ran to Alba's side. "You forgot this, my lady!" she said, holding up the Avalonian armour, which glimmered in the snow light. The girl eyed Lord Avallach defiantly, the pentacle on her cheek pulsing crimson in the cold air.

Elphin laid a hand across the strings of his

harp. "Don't hurt them, Father," he begged. "Please."

Lord Avallach frowned at the four friends standing defiantly in the midst of the Avalonian host. He looked at the wary ring of squires and damsels armed with snowballs and wooden swords. Unexpectedly, he began to laugh.

"*Faha'ruh!*" he said, turning his horse to join his people. "Maybe you youngsters have as much chance of finding the Grail as anyone else. In the meantime, if I see the druid's spirit I'll send him your way. Take good care of my son, Rhianna Pendragon."

"I will if you take care of my father's body, Lord Avallach!" Rhianna called after him. The Wild Hunt galloped off into the snowy wood with a noise like the sea crashing on a shore.

The thin wail of the captive souls lingered in the air for a moment. Then that, too, was gone.

Herd gone home, Alba said with a sad snort, shaking her mane.

Elphin sighed. "*Faha'ruh*, Father," he whispered, putting his harp away.

Rhianna knew she ought to be angry with Elphin, but she didn't have the energy. He looked so apologetic, and he'd stood beside her against his father in the end.

"Are you crazy?" She took out her tension on Cai instead. "Crashing in here after us like a wounded boar? That was the Wild Hunt! They might have taken your souls, too!"

Cai blushed. "Stupid horse smelled yours, and I couldn't stop him," he admitted. "Arianrhod said you'd gone out riding without your armour, so I offered to exercise him for

Sir Bors and said I'd give her a lift since he's big enough for two. I thought it'd be all right, only there wasn't time to find a saddle, and he's mad fresh after standing in his stall so long… Was that really the Wild Hunt?" He blinked at the sparkling cloud the mist horses had left behind.

"They won't be back, don't worry." Elphin gazed sadly through the trees. "Not until next year, anyway, and then only if the mists will open."

Cai looked a bit disappointed. The other squires were discussing what they'd seen in excited voices. Even Gareth seemed impressed, though he managed a haughty scowl for Rhianna and muttered something about hoping she didn't expect them to rescue her from every passing stranger just because she was King Arthur's daughter.

She smiled and warily touched Excalibur. The jewel still felt warm. She eyed Elphin. "You could have gone back with them, you know," she said.

Her friend shook his head. "Someone's got to help you find your father's champion knight and mend the Lance of Truth. I'm sorry about tricking you at the Round Table, Rhia. I was afraid Mordred's magic might hurt you, and I honestly thought the Hunt would be able to help us. I got scared when Mordred's shadow kept appearing, but I should have known nothing would frighten you into giving up Excalibur. Do you forgive me?"

"Of course I forgive you, you silly fairy!" Rhianna said. She punched him on the arm, making the others giggle.

"We're going after Sir Lancelot?" Cai brightened. "Really?"

"Can I come, too?" Arianrhod said. "You'll need someone to do your hair if you're going to meet the queen."

Rhianna grinned at her friends with a warm feeling in her heart. She'd like nothing better than to ride north to meet Sir Lancelot and her mother, though she had a feeling the knights would take some persuading to let her go with them. And first she had to do something about Excalibur: find a way to control her cousin's dark influence.

"No one's going anywhere until spring," she said with a laugh. "Let's get back to Camelot, shall we? If we hurry, we'll be in time for the midwinter feast."

◁ 14 ▷

Druid Magic

So ends my song of the Sword of Light
Secret of the Pendragon might
The hopes and fears of men now dwell
In the gentle hands of a brave damsel.

The midwinter celebration at Camelot promised to be almost as good as an Avalonian feast. Under Lady Isabel's watchful eye, the damsels and squires decorated the halls with holly and ivy and hung mistletoe in the doorways. Gifts of food had been arriving from nearby towns and villages all day, and the men had been out hunting in the snow. Servants hurried past with platters of roast venison and wild boar, trays of honey cakes and fruit pies, jars of mead and leftover Roman wine. There would be dancing later, so musicians practised tunes that echoed gaily down the corridors.

"Not bad for humans with only five fingers," Elphin said, listening to the music. "I could show them a trick or two, though."

"You can play your harp later," Rhianna told him. "I've something to do first."

Ever since their meeting with the Wild Hunt, she'd been thinking of Lord Avallach's warning about the forces of Annwn tempting her to use her sword for evil. She knew she had to find a way to get Mordred's dark spirit out of Excalibur before she hurt someone she loved.

But she couldn't think how, until Sir Bors reminded her that normally, after the midwinter mass, King Arthur would knight those squires who had completed their three heroic deeds that year. Tonight, since the king was not there, those who had fought in the battle would have their weapons blessed by the priest so they would be prepared for knighthood when it became possible again.

This gave her an idea. "Can I be blessed, too? I got Excalibur out of the lake, rescued you from the Saxon camp, and fought a dragon. That's three heroic deeds, isn't it?"

Sir Bors chuckled. "I suppose a blessing won't hurt. Nobody can call you a coward, that's for sure. But don't get any ideas, my lady. Damsels can't be knights. Leave your armour in your room tonight and act like a princess for once, huh? Nothing can hurt you in the chapel."

Rhianna grinned. At least he hadn't said no.

Determined to make a good impression in case her father's ghost was watching, she let Arianrhod dress her for the occasion in the green gown, now finished with gold embroidery. She even let her friend fix the jewelled net over her hair. She hung the pathfinder from Merlin's staff on a cord around her neck. Finally, she slipped the embroidered slippers on her feet and pinned a warm cloak around her shoulders. She left the shield and her Avalonian armour locked safely in the chest in her room. But she carried Excalibur in its battered scabbard hidden under her cloak.

As the sun went down on midwinter's eve, hundreds of candles were lit in the chapel, and everyone squashed on to the long benches to pray for the return of the light. The arched ceiling had been painted with blue and gold stars. The air smelled sweet like it did in Avalon. Torchlight from the castle wall found its way through a round window of coloured glass, casting splashes of red and gold on the floor. Looking up, she made out the dragon from her father's shield and banner. Her heart gave an extra thud.

"That's where we squires have to do our vigil before we're made knights," Cai whispered. "We have to kneel all night under the dragon and not turn around for nothin', or we'd fail the test."

"Did Mordred kneel in here as well, then?" Rhianna asked, a bit wary of meeting another of her cousin's shadows.

But Cai said fiercely, "Not all night, he didn't! The dirty sneak cheated. That witch-mother of his came and enchanted the guard's eyes so her precious little Mordred could get some sleep before he had to face King Arthur in the morning. Merlin said that's why he ended up a dark knight."

"Be careful, Rhia," Elphin whispered, frowning.

At the end of the mass, which sounded almost as beautiful as Avalonian singing, the squires who had fought in the battle filed up to the altar to kneel under the dragon. Cai went up first, very nervous. He dropped his dagger as he knelt, and flushed when Gareth sniggered. Rhianna quietly joined the end of the line and pulled out Excalibur.

Everyone turned to stare at her as she walked

between the benches, but she had eyes only for the priest standing at the altar surrounded by candles. He wore a grey robe that was so much like Merlin's, her heart gave a tug. On his head a bronze priest-crown glittered with strange symbols. She couldn't see his face properly in the shadows. He smiled at her as she approached and said, "Kneel, child, and let me bless your sword."

Her heart thumped as she knelt on the cold stone and held the Sword of Light upright between them. The white jewel brightened, making her dizzy.

The priest moved his hand over it and muttered something. The candle flames flared in a sudden draught. The hilt trembled in her grasp. Rhianna's neck prickled. What if she lost control and Excalibur turned on the priest?

But the priest lifted his hand with

a frown, and the sword stilled. "Druid magic," he muttered.

Rhianna sighed. They still needed Merlin – why did he have to get himself ambushed? "You know about souls, don't you?" she said.

The priest gave her a sympathetic look. "Yes, my child. Are you thinking of your father's? He was a good man, so it will have gone to a better place."

Rhianna shook her head, impatient. "I already know about my father's." She became aware of people starting to fidget and mutter on the benches behind her. "But where do druid souls go when they die?"

"I can't tell you that, child," the priest said carefully. "My learning lies elsewhere. Though some say druids can take the shape of birds and beasts—"

Her head spun. *Look for the dragon... Spirit transfer.* What if Merlin had sent his spirit into the shadrake to bring them his pathfinder? And she'd stupidly banished the dragon to Annwn! But Merlin was half Avalonian, and Elphin had told her Avalonians could not go to Annwn, so where...? Then she remembered the hawks attacking the shadrake during the battle. "The merlin!" She grabbed Excalibur with one hand, picked up her skirts with the other, and ran from the chapel.

The priest shook his head after her as sympathetic comments followed her into the night:

"Brought up in Avalon, you know...".

"Lost her father, poor child...".

"Bound to be upset..."

Rhianna hardly heard. Breathless, her slippers

wet with melting snow, she let herself into the hawk mews. It was deserted. Most of the birds were roosting, heads under their wings. Little ruffles broke the silence. No torches or candles burned in here. The hawkmaster must be afraid of the straw catching fire. Hoping the magic would still work after its blessing, she drew Excalibur. The white jewel blazed brightly, and warmth spread to her toes. She smiled in relief.

At first she couldn't see the injured merlin. Then a jingle came from the shadows at the back, and a familiar grumpy voice said, "You took your time, Rhianna Pendragon, I must say. I've been bored half out of my brain, tethered to this perch, waiting for you to bring Excalibur in here so I can talk to you."

"Merlin!" she whispered, pulling off the bird's little hood. "I was right – it is you!"

"Yes, yes, of course it's me. Who else would it be? The witch made a mistake when she set that shadrake on me. She always did underestimate me. I promised I'd meet you at Camelot, didn't I? I just didn't plan on losing my druid's body on the way." The merlin fixed a pale blue eye on her. "I picked the most obvious form available. Young Cai even told you what kind of hawk I am, but you were so busy dragon hunting I couldn't get your attention. What took you so long?"

"I've been a bit busy." Rhianna said, amused by the thought of the druid trapped in a bird's body.

"So I hear. Didn't I warn you not to use the sword?" the merlin grumbled. "I gather you've not only banished the shadrake with it, but also seen off Lord Avallach's Wild Hunt and spoken through the mists to your cousin Mordred! What possessed you, girl? Using the Sword of Light is no easy task. The more spirits it commands, the stronger yours needs to be to control them. Excalibur wore Arthur out, even before he stupidly knighted Mordred with it. I'm surprised it hasn't destroyed you."

Rhianna grimaced, remembering how tired she had felt after the battle, and how Mordred's shadow had almost tricked her into blooding the blade at the Round Table. "We've been looking for you everywhere!" she said. "I got your message at the stone circle, when you told me not to use Excalibur, but it didn't make a lot of sense. I just thought you meant not to blood the blade. Why didn't you warn me about Mordred's spirit being linked to the hilt so we can't use it against him? You lied to me!"

The bird fluffed out its feathers. "I planned to be with you when you retrieved Excalibur, remember. I thought Nimue and I would be able to deal with Mordred between us. I didn't want to scare you unnecessarily."

"Except you messed up by getting yourself ambushed and scaring us half to death by chasing after us in the body of that shadrake! You could have warned me you planned to use the dragon to bring us your pathfinder. We thought it was trying to kill us."

"Trying to control it nearly killed me," Merlin muttered. "But I didn't have much choice of bodies at the time. And then the creature insisted on speaking to you in dragon language… not that I suppose you understood very much."

"It made more sense than your silly message." Rhianna frowned. "Never mind. Lord Avallach says my father's body is not healing as well as it should, so now I've got to find the other Lights. Can you get Mordred's spirit out of Excalibur?"

Merlin sighed. "I'm afraid not."

Rhianna blinked at him. She could hardly believe that, after all their efforts, her father's druid had let her down. "Then Mordred was right! We've been half killing ourselves trying to get Excalibur to Camelot without blooding the blade, and all for nothing." Served him right if he was stuck in a bird's body, the old fool.

Merlin blinked a pale eye at her. "It wasn't for nothing. You've made peace with the Saxons, and that was well done. Arthur's ghost has obviously been looking after you. I hoped he might stick around, if only to protect you from the dark knight."

"He can't love me very much, then." Her heart

felt heavy. "Because I haven't seen him since we got into Camelot."

"Yes, that's unfortunate," the druid muttered. "He obviously doesn't think you need protecting now you're safe inside Camelot's walls. Ah well, you're here with Excalibur, that's the main thing. I'd hoped for a bit more support when we did this, but now is as good a time as any. Midwinter's a powerful time for magic. I should be able to open the mists even in this bird-brained body. Bring the sword over here and give me my pathfinder." He extended a claw.

"I'm not going to let you take it back to Avalon so Lord Avallach can unforge it..." Rhianna began.

The merlin beat its wings impatiently. "You're not listening, are you? Why did you think I brought you out of Avalon to help me look for Excalibur, when Nimue would have given it to me had I asked? It's true only a Pendragon can wake the spirit magic, and most men are frightened of it, but that doesn't stop others from handling the Sword of Light as long as they don't try to use it. I needed something to lure Mordred out of his lair so we could deal with him while he was still weak from his duel with Arthur. Something that would make him so furious, he'd forget to be careful... You, Rhianna."

She stared at the druid, chilled.

"You planned to use me as *bait* to catch Mordred? You should have told me!" She scowled at the small grey bird, torn between pity for its bedraggled feathers and an urge to chop off its infuriating little head.

The merlin eyed her in amusement. "And

would you have come with me so willingly if I had? No, don't answer that... maybe you would have. You're an unusually fierce damsel. Anyway, Mordred has sent his shadow after you several times and been defeated so he should be weaker now. I think we've a good chance of finishing him if we act fast. I'll open the spiral path to his lair. As soon as he comes through the mists I'll bind his spirit, and then the knights can deal with the traitor at their leisure. The path will only allow those who share a link with the sword to pass, so you should be safe enough as long as you keep hold of Excalibur. Go on, call him."

Her mouth dried. The last time Merlin had opened the spiral path, they'd used it to ride from Avalon to the world of men. What if Mordred came in the flesh, wielding the battleaxe that had killed her father? She looked about the mews uneasily. "Here? But—"

The bird fixed its pale eye on her. "What's the problem? This is Camelot. You've got Pendragon blood. Summon him! Or are you a weak damsel, after all?"

Her blood rose. Remembering how Mordred had killed her father, she planted Excalibur beside the merlin's perch and slipped the pathfinder from her neck. As the bird gripped the little spiral in its claws it began to shine, and so did the jewel on Excalibur's hilt. Mist curled outwards from the spiral, surrounding them with sparkling silver light. Everything beyond – the other hawks on their perches, the passage through to the stables, the door to the courtyard – became vague shadows.

She gripped the jewel firmly with both

hands and thought of her cousin's mocking smile. "Mordred!" she called, her voice echoing strangely as if they were underground. "Mordred, I know you can hear me! It's your cousin Rhianna. I've changed my mind. I've brought Excalibur for you. I'm in the hawk mews at Camelot. Come and get it."

At first she didn't think the spirit magic would work without the Round Table. Then the hilt shuddered in her grasp, the jewel warmed under her hand, and the shadows beyond the mist began to spin. Slowly at first, then faster and faster, until she felt dizzy. Finally, with a hiss like flames licking a damp log, the path opened – a glowing spiral leading from the merlin's perch out into the dark.

Rhianna's palms began to sweat. She tightened her grip on Excalibur, straining to see through the enchantment. If the dark knight came, she might only have one chance.

A draught stirred her hair, and she thought she heard someone whispering. "I am Rhianna Pendragon," she muttered. "I hold the Sword of Light. This is Camelot where I am among friends." But still nothing came down that path. Then she saw a movement in the shadows. She took a step towards it, then another…

Merlin sighed. "Either he's not strong enough to travel yet, or he can't hear you. Ah well, it was worth a try. At least we know we've got a bit more breathing space – where are you going?"

Rhianna was walking slowly around the spiral, holding Excalibur before her to light the way.

He killed your father, a voice whispered. *He killed King Arthur.*

As she ventured further out from the druid's perch, the whispering in her head grew louder and her hatred of the dark knight grew stronger, until she could think of nothing except taking her revenge.

"Rhianna Pendragon!" Merlin called behind her, beating his wings in agitation. "Come back here! Don't go to him alone, you foolish girl—" She heard the merlin take off, but it was leashed to its perch and could not follow.

She went faster now, running around the spiral, afraid the druid might close the path before she reached the end. She felt a bit sick. Shadows writhed and twisted about Excalibur. Darkness breathed across the back of her neck. She hoped Merlin was right, and nothing evil could touch her while she held Excalibur. Then she stepped out of the mist into a cold, dark place lit by smoky candles.

She stopped, blinking. She had come to a cave. In front of her, on a rocky bed, lay a boy only a few years older than herself. He had been terribly wounded. His right arm ended in bloody bandages where his hand should have been. One of his legs looked to be broken in several places. A sword cut had opened his cheek from ear to jaw, ruining his handsome face. But she recognised the green eyes, which were staring at her in alarm.

"How did you get in here?" He looked nervously at the spiral path, which sparkled in the corner of her eye.

"How do you think?" Rhianna said. "You're not the only one who can use the spirit magic."

When he realised she'd come alone, he relaxed slightly. "Ah, of course... you're not really here, are you? This is just your shadow. You can't hurt me."

"I wouldn't be so sure of that," Rhianna said, raising Excalibur and thinking of the black gauntlet that had gripped her wrist in the Saxon camp. "I hold one of the Lights. Want to test it?"

His gaze fixed on the shining blade, and his mouth twisted into a mocking smile. "So, cousin, you've decided to be sensible and bring me your father's sword, after all?" He pulled himself into a sitting position and extended his good hand.

Rhianna gripped Excalibur tighter as the hilt twisted in her hand. "No," she said, the hatred still burning in her veins. "I've brought it to kill you."

She couldn't see anyone else in the cave,

but Mordred wouldn't be alone, not with those wounds. She wouldn't have much time before his men came and found her here. Her heart banged. She stepped towards the shelf and raised Excalibur.

Mordred's eyes showed a flash of panic. Then he smiled. "Good try. But you're hardly going to manage what your father couldn't. Who helped you get here? Your fairy friend? Not bad for a first attempt, but the spirit magic can be dangerous when you don't know what you're doing." He jerked his good arm. The hilt jerked as well, turning the blade so that the sword swung down and almost sliced her leg open. Rhianna winced as it clanged off the rock, striking sparks.

The dark knight chuckled as he watched her struggle to control it. "Careful, cousin. Don't want to blood it, do you? That'll break the enchantment. Then you won't be able to get back the same way you came, and your friend will suffer too." He smiled at her expression. "Bet you didn't think of that, did you? So be sensible, eh? Give me Excalibur, and maybe I'll let you live as my hostage. There'll be a few conditions, of course, such as your friends opening the gates of Camelot to my bloodbeards, and surrendering the Pendragon throne to me."

Rhianna gritted her teeth and raised Excalibur again.

"The Pendragon throne belongs to King Arthur! You betrayed him. And Elphin didn't send me here. Merlin did. He's escaped your mother's trap and he's a druid so he knows plenty about spirit magic. I don't care about keeping the blade clean any more, because my father's not going to wake up if I take it back to Avalon, anyway. You told me that, remember?"

Her eyes filled with tears at the thought, and the sword shone brighter.

"All I have to do is call, and a hundred of my bloodbeards will come running," Mordred warned, scrabbling backwards on his bed. "You won't get out of here alive!"

"Maybe not," Rhianna told him, shifting her grip on the hilt. "But neither will you."

She'd never killed anyone before, but how hard could it be? He obviously couldn't walk far on that leg. One stab to the right place, like Sir Bors had shown her in weapons training, and then she'd run. If she couldn't get back along the spiral path, there had to be a tunnel leading to the surface. Excalibur would light her way. With Mordred dead, she could call on the strength of the other ninety-nine knights, steal a horse and gallop back to Camelot before anyone caught her…

The sword, influenced by the dark knight's spirit, was still fighting her, but Mordred seemed to be tiring. She took another step towards the rock bed, and her cousin paled. He groped for something on the floor.

Sweat trickled into Rhianna's eyes. It was no good. She needed more control over her sword to do this properly. She didn't want to make a mess of the death blow, but how could she stop Mordred's spirit from turning the blade? Lord Avallach had told them only unforging Excalibur would cleanse it of Mordred's influence. Then she heard Merlin's voice in her head: *Excalibur wore Arthur out, even before he stupidly knighted Mordred with it…* Maybe she could get her cousin's spirit out the same way it had gone in. She turned the blade and brought it down flat on Mordred's shoulder – first the left, then the right. "I unknight you!" she called in a ringing voice. "From this day you are no longer a Knight of the Round Table. Leave my sword!"

She had no idea if it would work, but Mordred shuddered and the hilt stopped twisting in her grip. A clean, pure wind blew through the cave as Excalibur's white jewel blazed, forcing back the shadows. The spiral path in the corner of her eye sparkled brighter. She thought she heard the druid's voice say, "Oh, well done, Rhianna Pendragon."

She grinned and took hold of the hilt two-handed. The sword no longer fought her, but pity stayed her final blow. Now she had unknighted him, she saw only a boy in pain, lying wounded and helpless in a dark cavern. She blinked the sweat out of her eyes. Would her father kill an unarmed boy?

She hesitated a moment too long. Mordred's hand swung up from the floor clutching a black mirror. He turned the glass so that the sword's light flashed back into her eyes.

She saw the stables she'd left behind in Camelot, the horses plunging and snorting in terror as large dark wings beat through the stalls. At first she thought it was another trick. Then, very faintly, she heard a frightened neigh.

Her head spun. "Alba!"

"That's right, cousin." Mordred laughed at her confusion. "You should have made sure your friends were safe before you brought the Sword of Light out of Camelot. The shadrake likes to hunt between worlds, and it's pretty angry now it's free of the druid's spirit. Without Excalibur, there's nothing to stop it attacking those you so foolishly left unprotected. I'd hurry, if I were you."

Now the dragon was swooping into her mare's stall. Rhianna raced back along the spiral, Mordred's laughter echoing in her ears. "Next time we meet I'll be armed and mounted, cousin!" he called after her. "Then we'll see how brave you are—"

She didn't hear what else he said, because the path closed at her heels as she leaped into the mews, Excalibur still blazing in her hand. Her spirit jerked, as if she'd woken up too fast. The merlin was flapping upside-down from its perch, screeching at her, but there was no time to stop and explain. She raced through the storm of feathers and along the passageway to the stables.

She looked quickly for the mist horses, and to her relief saw them safe and unharmed in their stalls, though they were shivering and sweating with fear.

"Where did it go?" she asked Alba.

"I AM UP HERE, PENDRAGON!"

The creature perched on a high beam, looking down at her with a glittering eye.

Rhianna warily pointed her shining blade at the dragon. "I thought I told you to go back to Annwn?" she said, opening the big doors to the courtyard so it could get out. "Go – and this time don't come back unless I say so!"

She ducked as the creature spread its great wings, afraid it would try to kill her now that Merlin's spirit no longer controlled it. But it swooped low over her head without touching a single hair and lifted its legs to avoid her sword.

"I CANNOT HARM A PENDRAGON," it boomed, "SO I WILL GO. BUT YOU DO NOT YET WEAR THE CROWN. WE WILL MEET AGAIN."

The dragon flapped out of the doors and away over the wall, where it vanished in a glitter of dark stars. Excalibur finally stopped blazing, and the jewel cooled under her hand. As the light faded, she saw a familiar figure in the courtyard smiling at her. He wore a ghostly crown that glittered in the starlight. *"Excalibur is yours now, daughter,"* he said. *"Use it well."*

Pleasure flushed through her. But before she could ask how long it would be before he returned to his body in Avalon, the ghost vanished into the night.

Alba nickered to her in relief. *Where have you been? I am glad you are back.*

Rhianna dropped the sword into a pile of hay and flung her arms around her mist horse's sweaty neck. "Oh, my poor darling… I'll never leave you unprotected like that again to go chasing after Mordred, I promise!" She shuddered as she realised how close she'd come to getting her horse and her friends killed.

Cries from the mews broke into her thoughts. A little guiltily, she remembered the druid. She went back through the passage and counted the frightened hawks, relieved to see the shadrake hadn't eaten any of them. She helped the flustered merlin back on to its perch. "Merlin? Are you still there?"

"Of course I'm here," said a grumpy voice. "Where else am I supposed to go? Back into that shadrake's body? No, thank you. Not when, every time you see that creature, you send it straight off to Annwn. You're lucky it didn't make off with my pathfinder again, or you'd never have got back from Mordred's lair… *I unknight you*? Wherever did you get that idea from?"

"I'm not sure." She grinned. "Worked though, didn't it?"

Merlin grunted. "Foolish slip of a girl! If you'd blooded Excalibur in there, you'd be in Morgan le Fay's clutches by now, and then what would we do?"

"I'm not that stupid." Rhianna said, remembering how close she had come to doing exactly that.

The merlin fluffed its feathers and fixed a pale eye on her. "Hmm… I'm not so sure. You took your time *unknighting* him. Still, at least you're safe from Mordred's influence now, which should make things easier when I'm fit enough to fly again. This body's such a fragile little thing. Who'd have believed it would come to this? I, Merlin, last of the druids, reduced to sleeping in a mews! You'll have to ask the hawkmaster if I can live in your room, of course. It's quite acceptable for a princess to have a small hawk, even one who doesn't gallop about the countryside hunting dark knights and dragons – hold out your arm."

"I don't think I want you in my room," Rhianna said as the bird hopped on to her wrist. "You tricked me! And you'll make a mess." But she fought a smile as she gathered up the jesses that tethered it to its perch. The merlin looked so small and pathetic that she couldn't stay angry with it for long.

Footsteps hurried along the passage towards them.

"Rhia?" Elphin said as he joined her. "Are you all right? We were worried when you ran out of the chapel like that! We saw that shadrake out in the courtyard. I think the mists opened again, but the creature flew off before I could fetch my harp." He handed her the sword, which he had rescued from the hay. "Is Excalibur…?"

"Excalibur's fine." She took the sword from the Avalonian prince and sheathed it, not yet ready to think about what had just happened. "I'm fine, too. I'll explain later."

The merlin's feathers were making her nose run. She made to wipe it on the sleeve of her dress, and someone thrust a square of soft material into her hand. Arianrhod. She smiled at the girl and blew her nose on the cloth instead.

"Who were you talking to, Damsel Rhianna?" Cai asked, puffing up last. "Your fairy horse again? At least you got us out of that chapel. The priest would have gone on and on otherwise, and I'm starving! The feast'll be starting soon, and we haven't even swapped presents yet... what are you doing with that silly hawk?"

The merlin had gone quiet since she sheathed her sword. The druid's powers must be limited, or maybe he was just too tired to talk any more. Rhianna spotted the little hood lying on the floor, next to the pathfinder. She grinned as she fixed it over the protesting merlin's head.

"Nothing that can't wait," she said, slipping the druid's spiral into her pocket. "Let's get out of here. All these feathers are making me sneeze."

Later, they exchanged gifts. In thanks for the green dress, she gave Arianrhod a net of silver for her hair that she'd found in one of the clothing chests. The girl's eyes filled with grateful tears. "It's beautiful. Lady Morgan never gave me anything," she whispered, trying to give it back. "It's much too fine for me, my lady!"

"Rhia," Rhianna corrected. "And if I've got to wear one then you can, too."

She presented Cai with a sturdy dun pony they'd rescued from the Saxon camp. "His name's Sandy," she said, as the boy patted the pony's neck with a delighted grin. "You can practise with your lance on him and show that stuck-up Gareth a thing or two in the joust."

Cai gave her a brow-band he'd made for Alba in the Pendragon colours, red and gold. Best of all, Elphin gave her a scabbard of soft red leather. "For Excalibur," he said. "I got it off a wounded knight I helped heal with my harp. I hope it fits."

Pleased, Rhianna tried the sword immediately. The scabbard slipped over the glimmering blade and the belt fitted around her waist as if it had been made for her alone. She gave Elphin a suspicious look. He smiled. "Nothing to do with me," he said. "That sword's magic, remember? I think it might have more power in your hands than Father thinks."

More than you know, Rhianna thought, remembering the fear in Mordred's eyes when she'd unknighted him. His words reminded her of a promise she hadn't yet kept. She got the biggest bucket she could find, filled it with rosy red apples from the feast table and took it into Alba's stall. "Don't eat them all at once or you'll get colic," she warned as the mare whinnied in excitement.

I am not stupid. Alba crunched one delicately from the top. *These are nearly as good as the apples back home.*

"I'll take you back to Avalon as soon as I can, beautiful one." As she patted her mare, Rhianna felt a bit guilty about her decision to stay in her father's world.

It is not so bad here. This stable has many fine stallions.

Rhianna laughed. "You be careful. I don't want you in foal by the spring!"

Finally, she gave Elphin the spiral pathfinder from the end of Merlin's staff and told him about the druid's spirit being trapped in the merlin's body. "So once you've persuaded him to teach you how to use it, you can go home whenever you like," she said.

Elphin's eyes swirled bright violet as he hung the druid's symbol around his neck. "I meant what I said to my father, Rhia. I'm not leaving you. We'll return together when we've found what we need to heal King Arthur, however long that takes."

"See?" Cai muttered to Arianrhod. "What did I tell you? They're inseparable."

Rhianna blushed. For once she could think of nothing to say. Should she tell her friends about her journey along the spiral path to Mordred's lair? Admit how she'd had the dark knight in her power but been unable to kill him? Already the memory was fading, like a bad dream.

While she hesitated, Elphin seized her hand and dragged her out of the stable. "Do you hear music?" he said. "Come on, Pendragon Princess. Let's show these humans how to *dance*!"

The moment passed. As they raced, laughing, back across the courtyard to Camelot's candlelit halls, she put Mordred firmly out of her mind. His wounds had looked almost as bad as her father's – he might even die of them before spring. Meanwhile, she was looking forward to practising misting with Alba and riding in her first joust. By then her mother should be back, along with the king's missing champion, and they'd have two of the Lights.

As for the boring old knights who wanted to shut her up in the Damsel Tower to protect her... Rhianna grinned and clenched her fist on Excalibur's luminous hilt... well, she had a whole winter to work on them.

A Gift For the Dark Knight

In his underground sanctuary, Mordred scowled into the cracked mirror. The happy squires and damsels, giggling and dancing in the candlelight, made him remember how he would never dance like that again. His shoulder still burned where the Sword of Light had touched him. He barely had the strength to raise his arm. He hadn't even considered that his cousin would dare come after him... though luckily she seemed to care more for her silly fairy horse than she had about killing him.

He shivered at the memory of how close he'd come to death. Ever since Merlin had brought Arthur's daughter out of Avalon, things had gone from bad to worse. And now his cousin had broken his knightly link with Excalibur. When he closed his eyes to try the spirit magic, his head spun so much he thought the world was going to end.

He clawed at his crippled leg in frustration. "Mother!" he snapped. "Stop it. I don't need to see this!"

The vision of Camelot faded and was replaced by his mother's image. As if to punish him, she looked more beautiful than ever. "You do need to see, Mordred my son," she said in her silvery voice. "You need to know your enemies."

"I already know them!" Mordred growled.

"My bloodbeards have been chasing my cousin and her stupid friends across the Summer Lands half the winter. She has the sword that should be mine, and her fairy friend has a harp that makes my head ache… more Avalonian magic! If it hadn't been for him I'd have made her blood the blade when she used Excalibur in the Round Table, and she'd never have been able to open the spiral path to reach me here. I won't get another chance now. She unknighted me! The druid tricked us!"

"Yes, that was unfortunate. It seems I underestimated Merlin, but he's learned his lesson with that shadrake and he's not much threat to us in the body of a bird. So they have the Sword, so what? The other three Lights are still ours for the taking. They've actually done us a favour in breaking your knightly link with Excalibur, because now they can't use it to find you. Cheer up, my son. I've a present for you. It's Christ's mass, after all."

Mordred winced. His mother's presents were not usually of the most welcome kind. "A decent horse to carry me out of here?" he said hopefully. "One that won't bolt at the first glimmer of Excalibur's magic?"

"In the spring," she promised. "This is just something to help while away the winter nights and keep you from getting bored."

The mirror flickered. Another wintery scene appeared, but thankfully not Camelot with its bright candles, happy people and ridiculous decorations. This time he saw a bleak fortress in a blizzard with black wings beating around it. A single window set high in the tower showed a flicker of candlelight.

He frowned. "Is that the best you can do? It doesn't look very comfortable."

"It's not supposed to be comfortable," his mother said. "You're not the one who's going to be living there. Look closer."

The image changed. Now he was looking into the tower room. A slender figure curled on a narrow bed. At first, seeing the freckles on her nose and her copper hair spread across the pillow, he thought it was his cousin again. He snatched up the mirror to throw it across the room. Was this his mother's idea of a joke? Rhianna's smug expression was the last thing he wanted to spend all winter looking at!

Then he realised this woman was older, her skin paler and softer. "The queen!" he breathed.

"She's yours, my son," his mother said. "Use her well."

Mordred fixed his eyes on the queen's image. He remembered all the times his Aunt Guinevere had called him a spoilt little boy. All the times he had seen her kissing Lancelot, but no one had believed him when he'd told, and his Uncle Arthur had thrashed him like a common squire for telling tales. "Can she see me?" he asked.

"If you want her to," his mother said. "Just speak her name, and put your hand over the mirror when you're done."

Mordred lay back on his rock and watched the queen for a long time. His heart quickened when she turned over and moaned in her sleep. He wondered what she was dreaming of – nothing very nice, if he knew his mother. He imagined waking her and telling her everything he planned to do to her precious daughter once he got out of here. But first he would let her lose all hope of rescue, would watch her pride crumble to despair in the lonely tower.

There was no hurry. He had all winter.

Mordred smiled and spread his hand to make the mirror dark.

Available now…

PENDRAGON LEGACY
BOOK 2

LANCE
OF
TRUTH

by KATHERINE ROBERTS

Read on for a preview of Rhianna Pendragon's
second thrilling quest…

October 2012 Hardback
ISBN 978 1 84877 271 7

THE DARK KNIGHT
SETS A TRAP

Mordred cast a final look around the cave where he'd spent the winter. Damp oozed from the rocky walls. His bed, where he had spent so much time suffering in the dark, would bear his bloodstains for ever.

He spat on it. "They will pay for my pain," he promised the shadows. "They will all pay."

He'd almost died of the wounds he had received last summer in the battle against his uncle, Arthur Pendragon. But now he felt stronger than before, in spite of his crippled leg and missing sword hand. King Arthur was dead, and Queen Guinevere his prisoner. His horse waited outside with his men.

It would only be a matter of time until he dealt with Arthur's daughter, the girl who stood between him and the throne.

Before he left this place, he had one more thing to do. He pulled on a black gauntlet with his teeth. Then he picked up the mirror his mother had given him so he could spy on the world of men. The cracked glass glittered as Mordred breathed on it.

He saw the tower that served as his Aunt Guinevere's prison. It was more comfortable than his own sanctuary, but the queen seemed not to appreciate it. She had tried to escape, and he'd been forced to send his bloodbeards to chain her to the bed. But she didn't know why she was a captive yet.

He'd been looking forward to this moment all winter.

He lit candles so she would be able to see him properly and put on his silver torque. He waited until she was combing her filthy hair and whispered, "Aunt Guinevere."

She jumped. The chain on her wrist clanked as her comb stilled. "Mordred," she whispered. "You can't keep me here forever! Lancelot will find me. Then he'll hunt you down and send your dark soul to join your mother's in Annwn for all eternity."

Mordred smiled, bored with her empty threats. He'd already made plans to take care of her champion. "Your precious Lancelot won't need to hunt me down. Unlike him, I'm not a coward who runs away from my fights. I've issued him a challenge. A joust to the death with you as the prize. You'll enjoy watching, I think."

She gripped the comb tightly, a flicker of hope in her eyes. "Lancelot carries the Lance of Truth! No knight has ever bested him in a duel. He'll kill you."

Mordred chuckled. "Oh, I doubt it. The lance is broken, as you well know. Without it, Lancelot's no greater than an ordinary knight. Whereas *I* will be fighting with the Sword of Light."

The queen went still. "Excalibur was returned to Nimue's lake," she said uncertainly. "The Lady of the Lake would never let a witch's brat like you have it!"

"No need to be rude," Mordred told her. "You really are behind with the news, aren't you? I suppose you've been a bit out of touch this winter, so I'll update you. My cousin Rhianna has got the sword back from Nimue, and will shortly be bringing it to me. You look puzzled, Aunt. Surely you remember your sweet baby daughter, with the cute freckled nose, the one you abandoned to the fairies? She's grown quite a bit since you last saw her. She's been in the world of men for some time now, looking for you. Maybe I'll let her keep you company in your tower. I wonder if you'll dare call me a witch's brat then?"

The comb clattered to the floor. The queen backed against the wall as far as the chain would allow and wrapped her arms around her body. "Oh God…" she whispered. "Rhianna… where is she? If you dare lay a hand on her—"

"Oh, I've already laid a hand on her,"

Mordred said, lifting his severed wrist and grimacing in memory of using the shadow magic. "She knows my power. Just not my plans for her – yet. We had a little, um, *misunderstanding* the last time we spoke, so I can't use the Round Table to send my message. But she should be receiving it any day now. Sometimes the old ways can be more persuasive, don't you think?"

The queen blinked and shook her head. "She won't bring you Excalibur! My daughter wouldn't be that stupid."

Mordred smiled again. "Ah, but you don't know her as well as I do. Believe me, she can be remarkably stupid once she gets a sword in her hand."

ABOUT THE AUTHOR

Katherine Roberts' muse is a unicorn.
This is what he has to say about her...

My author has lived in King Arthur's country for most of her life. She went to Bath University, where she got a degree in Maths and learned to fly in a glider. Afterwards she worked with racehorses, until she found me in 1984 and wrote her first fantasy story. She won the Branford Boase Award in 2000 with her first book *Song Quest*, and now she has me hard at work on the Pendragon series, searching for the Grail of Stars.

You can find out more about Katherine at www.katherineroberts.co.uk